I love th... me want to... n. My Mo...

One da... mystery... a real ch... ent it in and...

History... Carole... y to life. A...

I think... be in the mys... I always... hat is made u...

Grant...

I like t... at ages. ... favorit...

They a... rn a lot. There is always food which makes me hungry. I feel like I am there.

What Parents and Teachers Say About Carole Marsh Mysteries . . .

I think kids love these books because they have such a wealth of detail. I know I learn a lot reading them! It's an engaging way to look at the history of any place or event. I always say I'm only going to read one chapter to the kids, but that never happens–it's always two or three, at least!
–Librarian

Reading the mystery and going on the field trip–Scavenger Hunt in hand–was the most fun our class ever had! It really brought the place and its history to life. They loved the real kids characters and all the humor. I loved seeing them learn that reading is an experience to enjoy!
–4th grade teacher

Carole Marsh is really on to something with these unique mysteries. They are so clever; kids want to read them all. The Teacher's Guides are chock full of activities, recipes, and additional fascinating information. My kids thought I was an expert on the subject–and with this tool, I felt like it!
–3rd grade teacher

My students loved writing their own Real Kids/Real Places mystery book! Ms. Marsh's reproducible guidelines are a real jewel. They learned about copyright and more & ended up with their own book they were so proud of!
–Reading/Writing Teacher

"The kids seem very realistic–my children seemed to relate to the characters. Also, it is educational by expanding their knowledge about the famous places in the books."

"They are what children like: mysteries and adventures with children they can relate to."

"Encourages reading for pleasure."

"This series is great. It can be used for reluctant readers, and as a history supplement."

The Mystery at the Eiffel Tower

by Carole Marsh

Second Printing November, 2008

Published by Gallopade International/Carole Marsh Books. Printed in the United States of America.

Managing Editor: Sherry Moss
Assistant Editor: Erin Kelly
Cover Design: Michele Winkelman

Picture Credits:

The publisher would like to thank the following for their kind permission to reproduce the cover photographs.

© **Garrett Collins** *The Famous Chimere of Notre Dame;*
© **2005 JupiterImages Corporation** *Phantom Mask; Arc de Triomphe;*
Szalai Miki, Pécs, Hungary *The Louvre;*
© **Mike Tan | Agency: Dreamstime.com** *Eiffel Tower*

Gallopade International is introducing SAT words that kids need to know in each new book that we publish. The SAT words are bold in the story. Look for this special logo beside each word in the glossary. Happy Learning!

Gallopade is proud to be a member and supporter of these educational organizations and associations:

American Booksellers Association
American Library Association
International Reading Association
National Association for Gifted Children
The National School Supply and Equipment Association
The National Council for the Social Studies
Museum Store Association
Association of Partners for Public Lands
Association of Booksellers for Children

30 YEARS AGO . . .

As a mother and an author, one of the fondest periods of my life was when I decided to write mystery books for children. At this time (1979), kids were pretty much glued to the TV, something parents and teachers complained about the way they do about video games today.

I decided to set each mystery in a real place–a place kids could go and visit for themselves after reading the book. And I also used real children as characters. Usually a couple of my own children served as characters, and I had no trouble recruiting kids from the book's location to also be characters.

Also, I wanted all the kids–boys and girls of all ages–to participate in solving the mystery. And, I wanted kids to learn something as they read. Something about the history of the location. And I wanted the stories to be funny.

That formula of real+scary+smart+fun served me well. The kids and I had a great time visiting each site, and many of the events in the stories actually came out of our experiences there.

I love getting letters from teachers and parents who say they read the book with their class or child, then visited the historic site and saw all the places in the mystery for themselves. What's so great about that? What's great is that you and your children have an experience that bonds you together forever. Something you shared. Something you both cared about at the time. Something that crossed all age levels–a good story, a good scare, a good laugh!

30 years later,

Carole Marsh

Christina
Mimi
Papa
Grant
"Mystery Girl"

About the Characters

Christina, age 10: Mysterious things really do happen to her! Hobbies: soccer, Girl Scouts, anything crafty, hanging out with Mimi, and going on new adventures.

Grant, age 7: Always manages to fall off boats, back into cactuses, and find strange clues–even in real life! Hobbies: camping, baseball, computer games, math, and hanging out with Papa.

Mimi is Carole Marsh, children's book author and creator of Carole Marsh Mysteries, Around the World in 80 Mysteries, Three Amigos Mysteries, Baby's First Mysteries, and many others.

Papa is Bob Longmeyer, the author's real-life husband, who really does wear a tuxedo, cowboy boots and hat, fly an airplane, captain a boat, speak in a booming voice, and laugh a lot!

Travel around the world with Christina and Grant as they visit famous places in 80 countries, and experience the mysterious happenings that always seem to follow them!

Other Titles

#1 The Mystery at Big Ben
(London, England)

#2 The Mystery at the Eiffel Tower
(Paris, France)

#3 The Mystery at the Roman Colosseum
(Rome, Italy)

#4 The Mystery of the Ancient Pyramid
(Cairo, Egypt)

#5 The Mystery on the Great Wall of China
(Beijing, China)

#6 The Mystery on the Great Barrier Reef
(Australia)

#7 The Mystery at Mt. Fuji
(Tokyo, Japan)

#8 The Mystery in the Amazon Rainforest
(South America)

#9 The Mystery at Dracula's Castle
(South America)

#10 The Curse of the Acropolis
(Athens, Greece)

#11 The Mystery of the Crystal Castle
(Bavaria, Germany)

#12 The Mystery in Icy Antarctica
(Antarctica)

Table of Contents

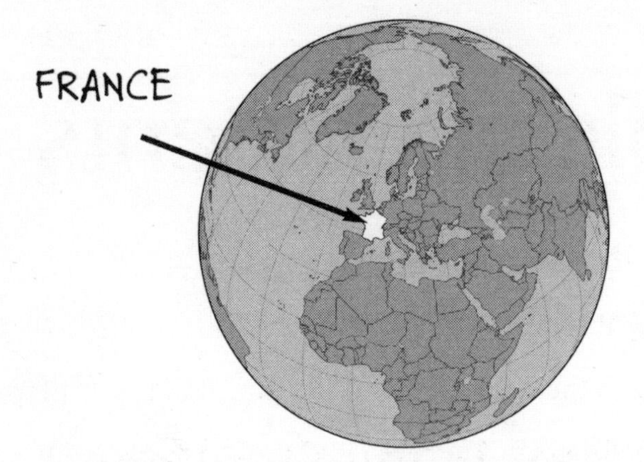
FRANCE

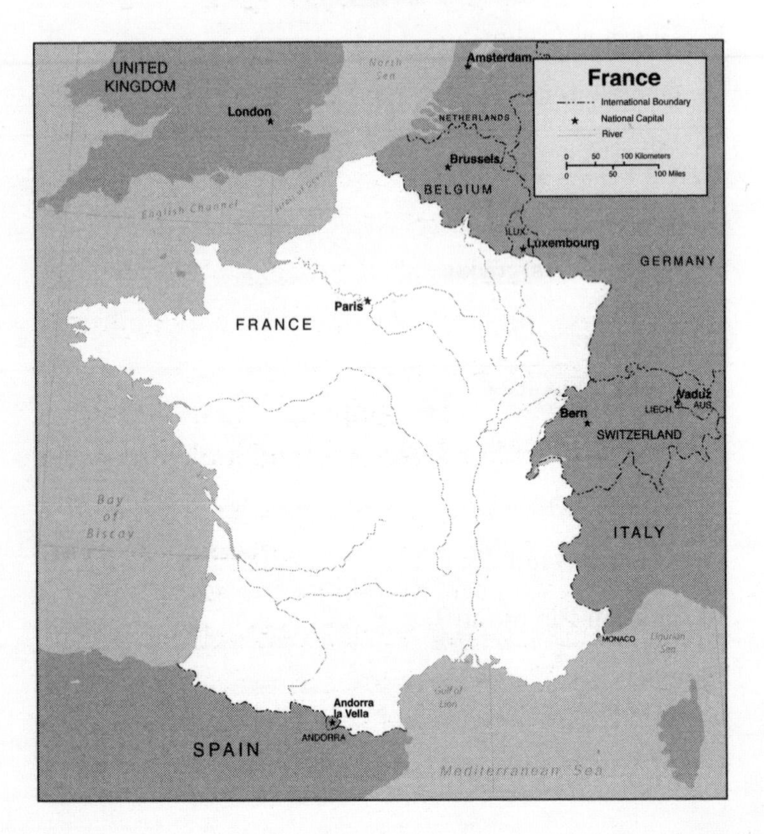
France
International Boundary
National Capital
River
0 50 100 Kilometers
0 50 100 Miles
UNITED KINGDOM
London
North Sea
Amsterdam
NETHERLANDS
Brussels
BELGIUM
English Channel
LUX.
Luxembourg
GERMANY
Paris
FRANCE
Vaduz
LIECH.
AUS.
Bern
SWITZERLAND
Bay of Biscay
ITALY
MONACO
Ligurian Sea
Gulf of Lion
Andorra la Vella
ANDORRA
SPAIN
Mediterranean Sea

Creepy Crêpes

I couldn't believe what I was seeing outside my window. The plane was spiraling faster and faster ... the ground was getting closer and closer ... the trees were getting bigger and bigger ... but I couldn't even scream! Why couldn't I scream?

Just then, ten-year-old Christina's head jerked back and whacked the back of her airplane seat. "Oh, my gosh," she gulped, "it was only a dream!" She rubbed her eyes and looked out the window just to make sure.

Satisfied that she had nothing to fear, Christina sighed with relief as the plane circled in for a landing. They were finally getting to visit Paris! She felt the excitement well up inside of her. She and her seven-year-old brother Grant would finally get the chance to meet their French pen pals, Marie and Jean-Luc, face-to-face.

Add that to the thrill of exploring a new city in a foreign country, and you get one happy girl, thought Christina to herself. "Mimi, how much longer till we get there?" she asked her grandmother, who sat beside her, a chic, black felt beret covering her short blond hair.

"It shouldn't be long now," Mimi replied, glancing at her watch. "I think Papa said we should land at the Charles de Gaulle airport around eight o'clock."

"Yippee!" shouted Grant, his blond hair in a mess. "Maybe we can get some of those creeps you keep talking about, 'cause I sure am hungry after this long plane ride."

"Crêpes [crapes], you silly, not creeps," laughed Christina, her stomach rumbling as she thought about a plateful of the light, thin pancakes, maybe even covered in a drizzle of melted chocolate. "I sure could use some too."

"Well, we'll see if we can find a good café after we meet your friends Jean-Luc and Marie and their parents. They probably know all the best restaurants in the city," said Mimi.

Looking out the window of the *Mystery Girl*, Christina glimpsed the point of the Eiffel Tower far ahead. A ray of sunshine caught the very tip-top of the tower. It sparkled like shiny tinsel on a Christmas tree. Somehow, she knew this would be no ordinary visit. After all, when she and Grant accompanied their grandparents, Mimi and Papa, on trips, they usually ended up getting caught in the middle of some sort of mystery. Christina silently wondered what this trip would bring.

* * *

Papa held Christina's hand tightly as she climbed down the steps of the little red plane named the *Mystery Girl*. It had been Mimi's birthday present to Papa. Mimi, who was a writer, and Papa used it to go on trips around the world so that Mimi could do research for her latest book. Often, Christina and Grant were invited to go along. The two kids loved to explore while the grownups did research. They always *tried* to stay out of trouble, but more often than not they would become involved in investigating some funny business or mystery that was going on. The brother-sister team always managed to save the day, but only after a few frights, a lot of confusion, and many good laughs.

The kids followed Mimi and Papa into the sprawling airport terminal. Christina noticed several moving sidewalk ramps covered in what seemed to be giant plastic tubes leading upward into the center of the building. “This way to baggage claim!” said Papa, waving them on with his arm. Christina gazed up in awe as they entered the plastic tunnel.

“I feel like a worm burrowing into the ground,” she said to Grant.

“This sure is some strange ground,” he replied, his big blue eyes looking from left to right and back again.

After they stepped off the moving sidewalk, the four waited at the customs checkpoint. When it came their turn, Christina proudly handed her United States Passport to the customs agent, who looked very official in his uniform and hat. As he stamped one of the pages, he mumbled something in French that Christina could not understand. After passing through the gate she rushed over to the baggage claim terminal.

“I see them, I see them!” shouted Grant,

waving and pointing at a boy and a girl holding a sign that said, "*Bienvenue à Paris, Christina et Grant!*" The boy was about Christina's age, and the girl a year older than Grant. Both children had dark hair and eyes and olive complexions, contrasting sharply with Christina's and Grant's blond-haired, blue-eyed looks. Behind the children stood two adults. The man and the woman were both elegantly dressed. Christina admired the woman's short, glossy black hair and her matching bright red high heels and purse.

As Mimi and Papa shook hands with the adults, Christina and Grant greeted the children with hugs and squeals. "It is so good to finally meet you face to face!" said Marie, with a charming French accent.

"We feel like we already know you so well from your letters," said Jean-Luc. The four children had corresponded through the mail for several months after Christina's schoolteacher had provided her with Jean-Luc's address and suggested she write to him. Christina had eagerly agreed, excited at the thought of having an international pen pal. Eventually, Grant and Marie had exchanged letters too, so the four already knew a lot about each other.

"Meet our parents," said Jean-Luc. "This is my father Cyril and my mother Dominique." He pronounced the names *see-real* and *doe-mee-neek.*

"Enchantée," [*ahn-shahn-tay*] replied Christina. Her teacher had taught her the phrase, which means "nice to meet you" in English.

"You speak very good French already!" said Dominique, with the same lovely accent as her children's. "We are delighted that you all could come for a visit to our wonderful city."

"And we appreciate your **hospitality**," replied Mimi. "It's so kind of you to let us stay in your apartment's guest room."

"Shall we find these tired travelers some food?" suggested Cyril with a smile and a wink. "You must be starving after such a long flight."

"Sounds like a plan to me!" said Papa, rubbing his tummy. "I could eat a horse!"

Bustling Bridges

After a ride into the city's center in Cyril's car, the four French and four American passengers stopped at a small sidewalk café for a snack. Christina soaked in the Parisian atmosphere. She was surrounded by new sights, sounds, and smells. She watched the bustling sidewalks, full of very fashionable women and colorful vendors' tables. Bicycles whizzed by, going almost as fast as the tiny cars that drove right next to them. Chatter in elegant French filled the air, mingling with music drifting from the café and the delicious smell of baking bread. The sidewalks looked very old, made not from smooth concrete but from small individual cobblestones placed tightly side-by-side. "It sure is easy to trip if you don't watch your step," said Christina.

Just as the words left her mouth, Christina heard a crash behind her. She whirled around to see Grant head over heels in the flowerbed next to the sidewalk. Jean-Luc quickly lifted him up, brushing the dirt off his shorts and pulling flower petals out of his hair. "I was just watching those tiny cars," Grant panted. "How can anyone fit in them?" Jean-Luc laughed. "I think we'll be keeping our eye on you," he said. "Now, let's find a safe place for you to sit down!"

The group was seated at several small, round outdoor tables on the sidewalk under the café's large awning. The waiter and Madame Dominique were having a conversation that Christina couldn't understand.

Grant nudged Jean-Luc in the ribs. "What's she talking about?" he whispered.

"She ordered crêpes and hot chocolate for everyone," he replied.

"All right! Creeps!" Grant shouted. "I told you..." Christina said sternly. Jean-Luc and Marie giggled behind their napkins. "I know, I know, it's crêpes, not creeps," said Grant. "Just kidding."

As the group eagerly devoured the delicious

French pancakes, Dominique gestured to the right, toward the huge, imposing stone bridge that crossed over the river Seine. "This is the famous Pont Neuf," she said. "Even though its name means 'new bridge,' it is the oldest bridge in Paris, built in 1578 by King Henri III. King Henri IV gave it its name. That's a statue of him in the middle there."

Christina and Grant gazed at the massive stone architecture of the bridge. It's more like a work of art than a bridge, thought Christina, glancing from the giant-sized statue to the small, semi-circular alcoves placed atop each solid pillar. People sat in the alcoves, some reading newspapers, some feeding the flocks of swarming pigeons, others just gazing downward at the greenish, murky waters of the famous river Seine that ran through the center of Paris. Christina knew from her social studies class that the island in the middle of the Seine was the Ile de la Cité, where Notre Dame stood. She could see its twin bell towers watching over the bustle of the streets below.

"You know what?" asked Grant, nudging her out of her daydream. "I want to ride a horse as big as the one that King Henri is riding!"

"I don't even know if horses that big exist," replied Christina, smiling gently.

"Speaking of statues," interjected Cyril, "have you heard about the statue that was stolen from the Louvre?"

"Oh no!" said Mimi. "What kind of statue?"

"It is a very valuable marble carving of a gladiator," said Dominique. "It only stands about half a meter high, so it would be very easy for someone to smuggle out under a coat."

"Oh, the metric system...I forgot," said Grant. He looked at Papa. "How big is half a meter?"

"About this high," said Papa, holding his hand about 18 inches from the tabletop.

But Christina wasn't listening to Papa's metric system explanation. She was staring at the bridge again. She could see a woman standing in the alcove closest to the café. The woman wore a full-length black trench coat even though it was a warm spring day. Her black hair was slicked back into an elaborate, twisty bun. She wore bright red lipstick and large black designer sunglasses that covered most of her face and made her look slightly like a bug.

She seemed to be staring in Christina's

direction. As Christina watched, the woman took a mysterious-looking, brown-wrapped package from under her coat. Then she quickly turned and walked away. Christina could hear her pointy-toed patent leather stiletto shoes clacking on the sidewalk. Now that looks suspicious, thought Christina. I wonder what she's hiding in that package.

Christina was again snapped out of her daydreaming by Marie patting her on the shoulder. "*Allons-y*! Let's go!" she said. "*Mama et Papa* are taking us to the Louvre museum!"

She grabbed Christina's hand and pulled her along behind the grownups, who were chatting about strange things like Etruscan art and Renaissance Italian painters. "This is the best museum in the city," said Jean-Luc. "You will get to see the Venus de Milo and the famous Mona Lisa!"

"Oh boy!" shouted Grant, breaking off into a run. "Ready or not, Mona, here I come!"

Lurking in the Louvre

"Oh, just look at this place!" cried a delighted Christina as the group made its way through the giant glass pyramid into the world-famous Musée du Louvre, or, in English, the Louvre Museum. As the escalator slowly descended, the pyramid caught the feeble sunlight and sparkled like a diamond. Christina craned her neck to look upward. Some clouds seemed to be gathering in the springtime sky. It looked as if they might be in for an afternoon thundershower.

At the bottom of the escalator, the group headed to the automatic ticket dispensers to buy their passes for the day. The machine beeped as it spit out the tickets. Grant giggled. "It's like those do-it-yourself checkout lanes at the grocery store," he squealed, "but more fun!"

Cyril motioned them over to an escalator. "We will have a look in the Denon Wing first," he said. "That is where the La Joconde, or the Mona Lisa lives." The group followed him up another escalator and through the kiosk where a woman marked their tickets. Marie impatiently tugged on Christina's hand and led her into the large room that lay straight ahead. Jean-Luc and Grant were right behind them. The adults followed at a more leisurely pace.

Christina gasped as she entered the room. Its soaring, arched ceilings and marble walls and floors took her breath away. She had never seen a more beautiful building. Her footsteps clicked and clacked on the inlaid marble floor and echoed off the walls. She looked over at Grant, who was practically bending over backwards to look at the ceiling.

"Can you believe how gigantic this room is?" he asked, wide-eyed with amazement. "I wish my bedroom at home were this big."

"But that would just mean more to clean," teased Papa with a wink. "Imagine trying to mop this floor. It would take all day long!"

"No thank you!" said Grant. "I think I'd hire a maid to do that."

Madame Dominique laughed as she began pointing out various paintings hanging on the walls. She talked about Renaissance painters and ancient Greek sculpture. Christina listened closely as Dominique pronounced exotic names of famous painters like Leonardo da Vinci, Carvaggio, and Vermeer. Bright blues, vivid purples, sparkling greens, and brilliant yellows leaped out from the canvases encased in huge, elaborate frames. Christina was amazed by the painters' talent. She glimpsed a portrait of Mary and Jesus, a portrait of a sad-eyed young man, and a stunning landscape scene. A sculpture of a marble head stared out from hollow eyes. Christina read the plaque attached to the marble stand. "*Jules César*," it read. "That's a bust of Julius Caesar, the famous Roman emperor," Dominique explained. Grant looked puzzled. "A bust? But he doesn't have a bust," he said. Dominique let out a hearty laugh. "A bust is a sculpture of the head and shoulders of a person," she said. Grant nodded, but still thought it was a strange name for a statue of a head!

Mimi and Papa had stopped behind a guided group of tourists. The children joined them. They listened to the tour guide explain how the Louvre was originally constructed as a fortress in 1190. Over the years, French kings had added buildings to the vast structure, which was eventually used as a palace. It became an art museum open to the public for the first time in 1793.

When the guide had finished her well-rehearsed speech, Cyril guided the group down an elaborate staircase and through a hallway. At the end, there was a small, round room with marble floors and walls. The ceiling was painted with scenes of flowers and chubby cherubs surrounded by gilt frames. In the middle of the room stood a glorious marble statue of a larger-than-life woman. Even though she was missing both arms, the woman had a certain mysterious beauty. Cyril explained that this was the celebrated Venus de Milo, an ancient Greek sculpture discovered on the Greek island of Melos in 1820. "Many consider her to be the great standard of feminine beauty," he said.

"Well, I think they're just plain wrong!" exclaimed Papa. "My wife here is *much* prettier than her!" he said, putting one arm around Mimi's shoulders and gesturing toward the statue with the other. Mimi blushed with embarrassment and delight.

"I must say, you do have a lovely wife, sir," Cyril agreed.

"And she's a real live person, too! She's not even made of stone!" joked Grant. "And she has two arms, which really helps when you're playing Frisbee!"

"No Frisbee playing in here, young man," chided the security guard with a wink.

Everybody laughed. Madame Dominique suggested that they head back into the Denon wing to see the Mona Lisa. Christina shivered with delight.

* * *

At the end of another large hall with an inlaid wooden floor stood a large crowd. People were swarming around, fighting for standing room. Cameras clicked and flashed every other second. A guard with a watchful eye stood a few feet away, surveying the scene to make sure nobody crossed the velvet rope that separated the visitors from the famous painting.

"There she is!" Grant shrieked with excitement. Christina playfully shushed him.

"She is as beautiful as ever," sighed Jean-Luc. "My sister and I first came to visit her when we were small children."

"She was painted in 1507 by Leonardo da Vinci, the famous Italian painter and inventor," said Marie. "Everyone is fascinated by her mysterious smile."

The children squirmed their way to the front of the crowd and stood behind the velvet rope. Christina gazed into the portrait's eyes. The woman's smile was indeed mysterious, maybe even a little menacing, like she was making fun of something. Even though she was beautiful, Christina thought she looked a little bit weird.

"I don't like the way she's staring at me," pouted Grant. "She gives me the creeps."

Christina felt people shoving her from all sides. "We'd better get out of the way and let other people have their turn to look," she said. As she turned to walk away, something on the floor caught her eye. It was a scrap of paper. She picked it up, and unfolded it. She saw unfamiliar words written in another language.

Si c'est vers la statue volée
Que vous voulez aller,
venez dehors vers une
antiquité

Must be French, she thought. "Look at this," she said, handing the paper to Jean-Luc. "Can you read it?"

Jean-Luc read the message out loud, the French falling off his tongue. It's such a beautiful language, thought Christina. She wished that she could speak it more fluently.

"Jean-Luc, tell us what it means in English!" said Grant.

"Well, it says..." replied Jean-Luc, pausing for a moment to think. "It says: 'If you want to follow the missing statue, come outside to an antique.'"

"Well, that makes no sense," said Christina. "Missing statues? Outdoor antiques? You'd think that all the antiques would be kept safely in this museum."

"It must be talking about the missing statue!" exclaimed Marie. "Wouldn't it be wonderful if we could find it and return it to its place in the museum?"

Oh no, thought Christina. Here we go again with another mystery! So much for a nice quiet tour of Paris.

"How do we *always* end up on these mystery-solving adventures?" she muttered under her breath.

"What did you say?" asked Grant.

"Oh, nothing," she said. "It just looks like we're in for some more detective work."

"I know what you mean," whispered Grant, catching his sister's meaning. "We're getting pretty good at this by now." *But would it be good enough?*

Odd Obelisks

The four kids gathered in a huddle. They had just discovered a mysterious clue that might lead them to the missing statue. Christina suddenly had an uneasy feeling. "The grownups!" she exclaimed. "We've lost them!"

"Mimi! Papa! Where are yoooooouuuuuu?" howled Grant.

"Quiet!" said Christina. "That guard didn't look too happy about that noise."

"Besides, everything will be all right," said Marie in a soothing tone of voice. "We agreed to meet the adults at le Chat Qui Rit café for lunch if we got separated."

"You mean we're just free to roam around Paris *by ourselves*?" asked a skeptical Christina.

"Certainly!" said Jean-Luc. "We grew up in

this city, so we know it very well. Our parents trust us to find our way around safely," he continued with a wink.

"Well then, we should work on figuring out this clue and see where it leads," said Christina.

"Let's see..." thought Jean-Luc. "It talks about an outdoor antique...I don't know of any antiques that they keep outside."

"It has to be something large and sturdy," said Christina. "Otherwise it wouldn't make sense to store it outside. Maybe it's talking about another statue."

"There are lots of statues outside the museum in the Jardin des Tuileries," said Jean-Luc. Seeing the American children's' puzzled looks, he added, "That's the large park outside the museum."

"But there are also lots of modern sculptures out there," objected Marie. "What if it's talking about something *really* ancient?"

"Could be," said Christina.

"What about the Obélisk?" asked Marie. "It was built in ancient Egypt and brought here to Paris in the 1800s."

"That must be it!" said Jean-Luc. "There is a drawing of something pointy on the back of this piece of paper! We should go to the Place de la Concorde."

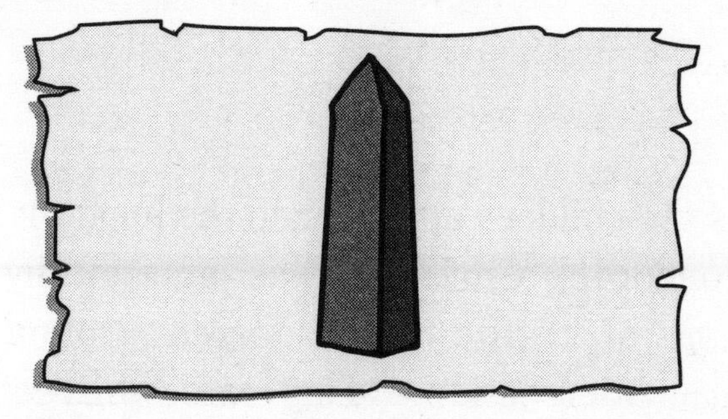

"Wait, hang on a second," said Christina.

"Yeah, what exactly is this octopus you're talking about?" Grant interrupted.

The group exploded with laughter. "**Obelisk**, not octopus, silly boy!" said Marie.

"Well, what exactly is an obelisk then?" asked Christina.

"It is a tall, four-sided carving of stone with a small pyramid on top," explained Jean-Luc. "The one in the Place de la Concorde, the Luxor Obélisk, is over 3,200 years old. It was built by the ancient Egyptians. It is covered in hieroglyphics. That's ancient Egyptian writing."

"Well, from the looks of the clue, we should probably head for this obelisk thing," said Christina. "It certainly is an antique and it's outside."

"We will go to the Place de la Concorde," said Jean-Luc, leading the group out of the museum.

* * *

As the children approached the huge Place de la Concorde, Christina was amazed by the amount of traffic that zoomed around the circular intersection. Tiny cars whizzed past giant lumbering tour buses and limousines. Nobody seemed to be paying attention to which lane they were in. It was every man for himself. Well, this certainly looks like an accident waiting to happen, thought Christina.

The red "Don't Walk" symbol changed over to green. Jean-Luc and Marie confidently led Grant and Christina through the jostling crowd on the crosswalk toward the center of the circle where the Obélisk was located. A beautiful fountain also graced the scene. It was round, with three tiers, each one cascading water down to the bottom. Fanciful black and gold mermaids and mermen held giant-sized fish that squirted jets of water out of their mouths. "I want a fish like that!" cried Grant. "We could set him up in the middle of the lawn like a sprinkler!"

"He might get mad and try to wriggle away if you held him like that," giggled Marie.

The children made their way to the base of the towering Obélisk. Christina craned her neck backwards to follow its shape all the way up to its pointy tip which pierced the cloudy Paris sky. Rows of mysterious symbols covered the sides. Those must be the hieroglyphs, thought Christina.

"I wonder if the pigeons ever sit on the very tip-top," **speculated** Grant, pointing to a flock of pigeons that were strutting around the fountain, cooing and pecking at the ground.

"If they do, they must have one of the best views of the whole city," said Jean-Luc.

"Forget the birds–what about that clue?" said Marie impatiently, bringing everybody back to reality.

"Well, it didn't really say much other than to come outside to the Obélisk," said Jean-Luc. "I really don't know what we should do now."

"Why don't we search around and see if we can find anything," suggested Christina. "You two look around the base of the fountain," she said, gesturing toward Marie and Jean-Luc. "Grant and I will take the Obélisk."

As the children spread out to start their search, Christina had the creepy feeling that someone was staring at her. She turned around abruptly. Nobody in particular was looking at her. There was only the huge crowd milling around the Obélisk. I must be getting paranoid, she thought to herself. But then, out of the corner of her eye, she noticed a familiar figure. As Christina whirled around to face it, the figure seemed to vanish in a flash of black. She could only make out the back of a long coat disappearing into the large group of people scurrying across the crosswalk. It must be that woman from the Pont Neuf, thought Christina. Wisely, she said nothing to the others. She didn't want to alarm them. Besides, she told herself, I don't want them to think I'm crazy!

"Over here! Over here!" Christina was pulled out of her reverie by Jean-Luc's shout. He was gesturing towards a spot over by the fountain. The group quickly gathered around him. "Look, another piece of paper!" he said, holding up another small slip like the one that Christina had found in the Louvre.

As Jean-Luc unfolded the paper, everyone leaned in closely to read what was written:

> Pour triompher dans votre quête,
> Chercher dans l'Arc une autre tête.

"Aww, man!" exclaimed Grant. "It's another one of those French clues...that I can't read!"

"Well, this one does not make much sense either," said Marie. "In English, it says 'In order to triumph on your quest, look in the Arch for another head.'"

"Another head?" questioned Grant. "I don't like the way that sounds. I like my own head just fine," he added, clutching his neck as if he was afraid someone would try to snatch away his head, blond curls and all.

"At least one part is easy to figure out," said Marie. "The arch it is referring to must be the Arc de Triomphe!"

"I bet you're right," agreed Christina, picturing the towering archway in her mind. "Let's head for the Arc!"

"But it could mean La Grande Arche de la Défense," objected Jean-Luc. "That's the other famous arch in Paris," he continued, referring to the gigantic modern arch which stood in the city's industrial section.

"It *has* to be l'Arc de Triomphe," said Marie. "*Regarde ici*, where the clue says 'triumph'– that could only mean the Arc de Triomphe."

"I believe Marie is right," said Christina. "I think we should head in that direction."

"Ahh, don't say 'head!!'" screamed Grant.

The kids laughed as they sped off towards the famous monument.

Uncanny Arches

The two brother-sister pairs strolled down what some call the most famous avenue in the world: the Avenue des Champs-Élysées. Christina gazed at the beautiful rows of trees that framed each side of the street. Her great-grandmother Dot had owned an oil painting of this very avenue. Christina had always enjoyed looking at that picture, imagining she was one of the fashionable French ladies taking a Sunday morning walk under her lacy parasol. The street was even more beautiful in real life despite the lack of sunshine. Even though it was spring, a chilly breeze blew down from the cloudy sky. Christina buttoned up her sweater against the cool air.

Marie was explaining to Grant that this

boulevard ran all the way from the Place de la Concorde, where the Obélisk was, to the Place Charles de Gaulle, where the Arc de Triomphe stood. "Napoleon Bonaparte, the famous general, had the arch built in 1806 to celebrate his victory at the Battle of Austerlitz," she explained. "It wasn't finished until 1836."

Christina could see the archway far in the distance. It looked blurry that far away.

"Maybe I should get Mom and Dad to build one of those in the back yard to celebrate my victories over math class!" joked Grant. "After all, I did make straight A's on my last report card," he bragged. "We could even put a giant waterslide underneath it!"

"That would be some kind of slide!" said Jean-Luc. "That thing is over 50 meters–oops, I mean about 164 feet–high."

"How do you two know so many facts and figures about Paris?" questioned Christina. "I know you've lived here all your lives, but you know so much already. I'm impressed!" she concluded.

"Well, we *Parisiens* are very proud of our city and its history, so we are taught lots of things about it in school," said Marie. "Besides," she continued, "our mother used to work as a tour guide. Sometimes as small children, we would go with her to work. We learned a lot of facts that way."

"That must be such an interesting job," said Christina. "I bet your mom met a lot of interesting people."

"Yes, it was a wonderful job," explained Marie. "Our city is so beautiful, who wouldn't want to see all these incredible sights every day? But you know what, " she continued, "I know she would love to be a writer like your *grand-mère* Mimi."

"Yeah, that way you would get to go on all kinds of cool trips with her," said Grant.

The conversation dwindled as the two American children took in the sights of the world's most famous boulevard. Christina gazed at the tall, elaborate buildings, the crowds of people rushing around, the sidewalk cafés, and most of all, the shops. Beautiful women and their handsome escorts strolled in front of the large storefront windows filled with expensive-looking fur coats, evening dresses, leather jackets, and silk blouses. A men's store display showed stiff tuxedos and collared shirts in every color of the rainbow.

Christina paused in front of a small jewelry store to get a closer look at the display. Diamonds and rubies and emeralds and sapphires sparkled up at her from the glass cases lined in black velvet. Rings, earrings, necklaces, and bracelets glittered everywhere. It was like Aladdin's treasure cave come to life!

"Come on, slow-poke!" said Grant. "Nobody cares about all these dress-up clothes! Except maybe *girls*," he muttered under his breath.

Christina hurried to catch up with the group. She couldn't wait until she was old enough to go shopping and carry big bags filled up with famous designer clothes. She was brought out of her glamorous daydream by Marie.

"We should hurry up if we want to make it to the Arc before lunchtime!" Marie said. "We cannot be late or else the adults will worry."

The children picked up speed, slicing through the crowds. "*Excusez-moi! Pardon!*" Jean-Luc and Marie said when they accidentally bumped into someone. Within a few minutes they were standing at the foot of the giant arch. It soared above their heads in graceful curves. The surfaces were covered in elaborate carved scenes. Lists of names were inscribed on the inner surfaces.

"Look, these are battle scenes," said Jean-Luc, gesturing toward the carvings above their heads, "and these are the names of the emperor Napoleon's Imperial soldiers," he continued, pointing to the lists of names.

"Let's go upstairs!" exclaimed Grant impatiently. He was heading toward a narrow stone staircase. The others followed him up the steep steps, holding onto the handrail.

Grant was jumping up the stairs two at a time. "Whew! Slow down!" puffed an out-of-breath Christina. "We'll get there soon enough." As she spoke, the group emerged out onto the observation platform of the arch. A few people were wandering around, taking pictures and gazing over the fence at the fantastic view of the city.

Christina climbed up on the stone ledge and peered out over the railing. The scene took her breath away. She felt like she could see all of Paris spread out below her. She gazed at the people, as tiny as ants, walking on the ground, and the toy-sized cars moving along the twelve streets that spread out like a star from the base of the monument. The wind whipped her hair back from her face. In the distance, she saw the pointy spire of the Eiffel Tower. It seemed to pierce through the blanket of grey clouds covering the Parisian sky.

She felt a tap on her shoulder. It was Jean-Luc. "What about this head we are supposed to be looking for?" he asked. A chill crept down Christina's spine. Was it from the cold breeze, or was it from the mention of a head? She carefully climbed down from her perch.

"Let's look around," she said bravely. Marie and Grant were chasing each other and playing hide-and-seek. She scanned the floor in front of her. Nothing so far, just bits of trash and gum wrappers. And pigeons. "This city is overrun by pigeons," she said softly to herself. Right on cue, as if he had been listening, a pigeon swooped down and landed right in front of her.

"Prrrrr! Prrrrr!" he cooed, bobbing his head. Christina noticed that he held something in his beak. He dropped it with a clink and flew away into the wind. She stooped down to pick it up. It was a coin!

"Come look, everybody!" she cried. "I think I found something!" As the others rushed over to her, she turned the coin over and examined it. On one side, there was a man's profile, and on the other, what looked like an open treasure chest overflowing with jewels and gold.

Marie took the coin and inspected it. Her eyes lit up. Pointing to the profile on one side, she exclaimed, "This must be the head that the clue was talking about!"

"Thank goodness!" said Grant with a shudder. "I'm glad it wasn't another kind of head...say, somebody's missing head!"

"Oh, cut out the spooky stuff!" said Christina. She was apprehensive enough already. "So we found the head," she said, "but what about this treasure chest full of jewels on the other side? What does that have to do with a missing statue?"

"I don't know about that," said Jean-Luc with a groan, "but I do know one thing. If we don't leave *now*, we will be late for lunch!"

Ghostly Galleries

The kids arrived–slightly disheveled–at the small sidewalk café just on time. "I think we must have beaten the adults," said Jean-Luc. "I don't see them anywhere."

"Well, that was lucky," said Grant. "Papa hates for us to be late. And I hate to be late for any meal," he added, patting his tummy. Christina didn't hear their conversation. She was too engrossed in the café itself. Delicious, unfamiliar smells wafted out onto the sidewalk. Christina's stomach rumbled, reminding her of how hungry she was. She looked at the wooden sign hanging up outside. "*Café du Chat qui rit*," it read. A picture of a large, grinning black cat sat on top of the lettering. His tail curled down and around the words.

"What does that mean?" she questioned Marie, pointing toward the sign.

"The Laughing Cat Café," Marie replied. "This is one of our favorite places to come to eat lunch. They have delicious desserts," she winked.

"Well *bonjour*!" Mimi's cheery voiced greeted the children.

"*Les voilà*!" said Madame Dominique. "There they are!"

"I'm impressed! They beat us!" said Papa.

A waiter in a long white apron came to seat them at a table inside. Christina sat next to Mimi. That way, she could gaze out the window and watch the people going by. A strong wind was blowing, fluttering the scarves at an outdoor merchant's table across the street. The café's awning flapped back and forth.

"Look over there," said Jean-Luc, pointing to the roof of a building across the way. "You can see the spire of the Eiffel Tower from here!"

Christina could indeed see the pointy spire sticking up behind the building. She wondered how high up it was. Her tummy growled again, bringing her thoughts back down from the tip-top of the tower. She glanced at the menu.

Unable to make sense out of the French, she turned to Jean-Luc. "I think I'll let you order for me," she said. "Pick something yummy!"

"Then we will have a *croque-monsieur*!" he said, turning to the waiter and placing their order. "It is the specialty of the house," he said to Christina.

"Now what exactly am I going to be eating?" she asked skeptically.

"Oh it is like a...how you say in America...fried cheese sandwich," said Marie.

"You mean grilled cheese? My favorite!" cried Grant. "When you said 'crock,' I was sure hoping you didn't mean 'crocodile!' I heard we might eat strange things in France!"

Marie smiled at Grant. "Yes, grilled cheese, that is what I meant," she said. "A *croque-monsieur* is grated cheese melted on a slice of toasted bread. There are lots of different ways to prepare them," she explained.

"Some people like to fry an egg on top," added Jean-Luc. "When they do that, it is called a *croque-madame*."

"Ooo, looks delicious!" exclaimed Christina as the waiter set her food down. She took a bite, and closed her eyes in delight. "Mmmmmmmm, this is great!" she said, as she stuffed her mouth so full she looked like a squirrel storing nuts for the winter.

"I'm glad you like it," said Jean-Luc. "It is my favorite lunch."

"How was the rest of your morning, kiddos?" asked Mimi, looking up from her big green salad.

"We took Christina and Grant down the avenue des Champs-Elysées to l'Arc de Triomphe. We climbed to the top and looked out over the city," answered Marie.

"What did you do, Mimi and Papa?" asked Grant through a mouthful of *croque-monsieur*.

"We took a stroll though the Jardin de Tuileries outside the Louvre," said Cyril. "It was quite pleasant, but a little windy," he continued.

"It looks like it is getting worse," said Madame Dominique, gesturing toward the window. The wind was whipping around the street corners. People were turning up their coat collars. Christina saw the street merchant closing up his booth.

"Do you have plans for after lunch?" asked Jean-Luc, as he wiped his mouth with a napkin.

"We thought that we would make a trip to the Galeries Lafayette," said Madame

Dominique. "After all, it is one of the largest and most famous department stores in Paris," she continued.

"I'm excited about shopping for an evening gown and some matching shoes!" said Mimi with a big grin. "Maybe we could find a dress for you to wear tonight, Christina."

"Tonight? What's going on tonight?" asked Christina, confused.

"Oh, we forgot to tell them!" laughed Madame Dominique. "We made dinner reservations at one of the best restaurants in the city, the Jules Verne, on the second observation floor of the Eiffel Tower."

"Oh, how exciting is that!" exclaimed Christina. "It sounds so cool! Do we have to get dressed up?"

"Yes, it is a rather formal setting," said Cyril. "I'm afraid that means a coat and tie for the young gentleman here." He gestured teasingly towards Grant.

"Yuck, dress-up clothes! I hate ties!" exclaimed Grant with disgust. "I think I'll skip the fancy part and eat my dinner in the kitchen."

"I think the food will more than make up for the tie-wearing part. This restaurant is home to some of the finest cuisine in Paris," said Cyril.

"Our reservation is at seven o'clock sharp," said Papa. "We can't be late!"

"You are more than welcome to stop by our apartment to change clothes before you leave for the restaurant," said Madame Dominique graciously. "Your luggage should already be there."

"Be sure to unpack neatly," said Mimi. "And don't forget to hang up your clothes! We don't want you two to be all wrinkly. Oh, and don't look in my bags," she continued. "I just might have a surprise in there for you." She winked secretively at Papa.

"That means no sneaking into Mimi's makeup case!" said Grant to Christina.

"Hey, I'm not the one who used her lipstick and eyeliner for war paint!" she teased back.

Brother and sister dropped their banter in favor of the dessert that the waiter had just set in front of them.

"Oh, *tarte tatin*!" said Marie with delight. She spooned what looked to Christina like some white, gooey stuff over her slice of pie.

"It's like an upside down apple pie," explained Jean-Luc when he saw Grant's skeptical look. "Don't worry, it doesn't have snails in it."

"What is that white stuff?" asked Grant.

"That is *crème fraîche,*" said Marie. "It tastes kind of like sour cream. Try some," she insisted, spooning a generous portion over Christina's slice of pie. Here goes, she thought. I might as well be adventurous. To her surprise, it was a fabulous taste! The tart *crème fraîche* was a perfect complement to the warm, caramel flavor of the apple pie. Before she knew it, she had cleaned her plate.

"Oh, Grant, look at you," cried Mimi. "You look like puppy with milk on his nose." Trying to smell the *crème fraîche* before he tasted it, Grant had gotten a little too close and dipped his nose in the white *crème.* Grant grinned and quickly tried to lick the cream off his nose with his tongue. The children roared with laughter. "Okay, that's enough," Mimi giggled. "We can't take you anywhere!"

When they had all finished their desserts, Madame Dominique asked, "Are we ready to go to the Galeries?"

Papa sat back from the table with a contented sigh. "I think I just might have to buy some bigger pants after that meal!" he joked.

As the group left the café, Christina couldn't help but notice a familiar figure sipping a cup of steaming coffee at a corner table. She couldn't tell because of the shadow over the woman's face, but it looked an awful lot like the same woman Christina had seen at the Pont Neuf and the Place de la Concorde. Either she's following us, or I really *am* imagining things, thought Christina. She truly hoped it was just her imagination.

* * *

The group stepped off the street into the giant department store. "This windstorm is getting worse and worse!" said Madame Dominique, straightening her disheveled hair.

"Let's hope it stops soon. I almost lost my beret!" joked Mimi. "Welcome to Galeries Lafayette!" said Cyril, gesturing grandly with his arms. "Anything you need, you will find it in here!" he said. A young man in a dark suit and shiny black shoes approached him and spoke to him in a low voice. "*Non, merci,*" he said to him.

"Whoa, you must shop here a lot. They

already know you here," said Grant.

"No, actually this is where I work," said Cyril with a smile. "That was Gérard, one of my assistants. He came to see if I needed anything."

"Your dad has my dream job," said Christina to Marie. "I would *love* to be the head of a giant department store like this. You would get to wear all the latest fashions!"

"It is fun to come to work with *Papa*," said Marie. "Sometimes I try on some of the new clothes that come into the store," she confessed with a giggle.

"I am going to take your *grand-mère* to look for an evening dress," Madame Dominique said to Christina. "Why don't you take your friends to the toy department?" she said to Jean-Luc.

"Sounds good to me," said Grant. He waved his hands around and made zooming noises as if he were flying imaginary toy airplanes.

"Wait until I show you the hats upstairs!" Marie was saying to Christina. But Christina wasn't listening. She had found the strange-looking coin in her pocket. She took it out and looked it over again. She noticed some small letters engraved below the man's profile on one side. "Lafayette," it read. That's a strange coincidence, she thought. Here we are in the Galeries Lafayette. She turned the coin over and examined the treasure chest. Miniscule gemstones and coins spilled out over the edges of the tiny chest. They reminded Christina of the jewelry store window she had seen on the Champs-Elysées...

"That's it!" she exclaimed, bewildering the others. "Jewelry!"

"What is this about jewelry?" asked Jean-Luc, who was thoroughly confused.

"I think I figured out the clue on this coin," said Christina. She went on to explain how she had found the name "Lafayette" engraved underneath the man's portrait, and how the treasure chest had reminded her of the jewelry store. She paused a moment to let her explanation sink in.

"I think you may be right," said Jean-Luc quietly. "Let's go to the jewelry department and see what we can find."

* * *

The gang stepped quietly off the elevator. "Be quiet," said Marie. "The clerks might not like the idea of a bunch of kids sneaking around their precious valuable gemstones." Crouching down to avoid being seen, the group sneaked slowly toward the center of the room. A woman walked by, carrying a large cardboard box. The children ducked down behind the glass jewelry display cases.

"That was close," whispered Christina, breathing a sigh of relief.

Jean-Luc poked his head up over the counter. "The clerk has her back turned. Let's go!" He waved the group on with his arms. This floor of the giant department store was eerily quiet. There seemed to be only the kids and the clerk around. Maybe the jewelry is so expensive that no one can afford to shop here, Christina joked to herself. As she passed by another row of display cases, she glanced inside at the sparkling gold and silver chains and the rings encrusted with multicolored precious stones. No wonder they don't want people like us sneaking around, she thought. Those things must be worth a fortune.

Crack! "Ouch!" whispered Grant, doing his best to stifle a yelp of pain and surprise. He had stumbled and hit his elbow on the sharp corner of a counter. Christina cautiously sneaked over to where he had tripped. She saw another slip of paper on the floor. She picked it up and stuffed it in her pocket.

"Uh-oh," said Grant, pointing upwards. The angry face of a clerk stared down at them from above the counter.

Christina gulped nervously. "This can't be good," she said in a low voice. The clerk started yelling furiously and gesturing towards the stairwell. Christina was suddenly glad that she didn't speak French. She didn't really want to know what kind of things he was saying. The group of kids ran for their lives down the stairs and didn't stop until they were out on the street.

What the children didn't see was the clerk pick up a nearby phone to make a call. After he spoke a few angry words, he hung up the phone quickly and hurried back to the jewelry counter. *But whom did he call?*

Menacing Métro

Once the kids were outside on the street, they collapsed, panting, from their hasty exit. "That's the last time I *ever* go shopping!" huffed Grant in between gasps of air.

"I hope we didn't get you two in trouble with your father," Christina apologized to Jean-Luc and Marie. "Surely all the clerks know who you are."

"I don't think that he had enough time to get a good look at our faces. Otherwise he might have recognized us and...well, not yelled," said Jean-Luc sheepishly.

"Oh well, it's over now," said Christina. "Look what I found just before we ran out," she continued, reaching into her pocket for the piece of paper that she had found on the jewelry department floor. She smoothed out the wrinkles and handed it to Marie. "It's probably written in French like the rest of them were."

Marie looked carefully at the piece of paper. She wrinkled her eyebrows. "Actually, it's not written in anything," she said.

"It's blank? What a bum clue!" complained Grant, disappointed.

"No, it's not blank," said Marie, handing him the piece of paper. "Look for yourself."

The group crowded around Grant and examined the clue. In the middle of the paper was a tiny drawing. "It's another head!" howled Grant.

"It looks like..." said Christina.

"Vincent Van Gogh!" she and Jean-Luc exclaimed in unison.

"I recognized the picture as a copy of one of his self-portraits. We studied him and his paintings in art class in school," Christina explained modestly. She didn't want to sound like a know-it-all.

"Very good eye!" said Jean-Luc. "I have seen this portrait in person before," he continued. "It is kept in the Musée d'Orsay."

"Oh, the museum with all of the

Impressionist paintings?" asked Christina. She had studied this particular style of painting in the same art class that she had mentioned earlier.

"*Oui*, that is correct," said Marie.

"There are works from other famous painters in the museum, too," added Jean-Luc. "Have you heard of Claude Monet and Edward Manet?"

"I think I have, but it's confusing," said Christina. "You have too many Monets and Manets!"

"Yeah," Grant piped up, "If I had some mayonnaise, I'd make a sandwich."

Christina was not thinking about food. "I think the Impressionist style is just beautiful," she said. "I love the way it captures the light in each scene. It's like the artist took a picture in his mind and then copied it onto the canvas."

"Ok, quit with all the I-know-everything talk!" Grant said to his sister. He hated it when she got into these "I'm smarter than you are" moods. She elbowed him in the ribs so he would be quiet. "Hey, Grant, here's something you'd be interested in," she said. "Did you know that Van Gogh cut off his ear?"

"Why, so he didn't have to listen to his sister anymore?" Grant shot back, rubbing his ribs.

"Okay, I think we all know what this means," said Jean-Luc, interrupting the siblings' squabble.

"Right," agreed Marie. "It's time to go to the Musée d'Orsay!" she said.

* * *

"It is easy once you get the hang of it," Jean-Luc said in a comforting voice. "You will learn it very quickly."

Christina was slightly nervous about her first trip on the *Métro*, Paris' underground subway system. It seemed so intimidating, going underground into the mysterious system of trains and tunnels. However, Jean-Luc and Marie had been reassuring, guiding them down the stairs into the station, examining the giant map on the wall, buying tickets, and finally striding confidently down one of the many halls toward the train platform.

Before they entered the system of hallways that led to the various train platforms, the French children had stopped at a row of turnstiles. They fed their small purple tickets into the slot of a machine which stood next to the turnstile. The machine made a grinding noise and spit out the ticket through another slot. Jean-Luc showed them the purple mark that the machine had stamped onto the ticket. "This proves that you paid for your ride," he explained.

After having their tickets stamped, Christina and Grant followed their friends onto the platform to wait for the train. A large crowd of people stood waiting. "Stick close together," advised Marie. "The cars can get very crowded, and we don't want to get separated."

"In case we do get lost from each other," said Jean-Luc, "remember to get off the train on the third stop. The name of the station is *Solférino*."

Christina looked around the platform. The ceiling was arched in a semi-circle shape. The walls were covered in shiny white tiles. Over the edge of the platform, the track stretched out and disappeared into a tunnel as black as midnight. Giant advertising posters on the walls featured models showing off elegant fashions, announcements for concerts, and movies. Christina recognized some of the films as American. It would be funny to see a movie with subtitles, she thought. It must be hard to try to watch the action on the screen *and* read the actors' words at the same time! Maybe it gets easier when you are older, she thought.

A distant rumble shook the station's floor. "Here it comes!" said Jean-Luc. "Be ready to push your way on quickly. The stop only lasts about 30 seconds," he advised. "If you don't hurry, you might get left behind."

The children edged their way through the crowd towards the train, which was now pulling into the station and slowing down. The people on board were standing up and collecting their baggage, preparing to exit the cars. The train stopped with a hissing noise. A beep sounded, and the sliding doors squeaked open. Christina and the others pushed and shoved their way onto the car. Another beep sounded and the doors slid closed. There were plenty of people who hadn't made it onboard still waiting outside on the platform.

The children were squished against the back wall of the car. The train started to move with a forward lurch, causing the kids to stumble. Christina almost fell down. After regaining her balance, she followed Marie, who was edging her way towards the center of the car. Both girls grabbed onto the pole that was placed there for support. It seemed like everybody who didn't have a seat was clustered around the pole, desperately hanging onto it for balance as the train swerved and lurched around curves in the black underground tunnel.

Christina looked through the forest of grown-ups' legs. She saw Jean-Luc on the opposite end of the car, hanging onto another pole. Grant must love this, thought Christina. I bet he's pretending to be a fireman sliding down a pole in the station. She looked around to see what Grant was doing. She didn't see him with Jean-Luc. He must be sitting down, she thought. She stood on tiptoe and craned her neck so she could look over the rows of benches. No curly blond head. Where was Grant? "Grant, where'd you go?" she called out. She got funny looks from the adults around her. Oops, it's the English, she thought. She turned to Marie and asked, "Have you seen Grant?"

"*Non,*" said Marie. "Is he missing?"

"That's what I'm trying to figure out," said Christina, who was beginning to get concerned. "I hope we didn't lose him back there at the station. There were so many people getting on and off the train..."

"Let's go ask Jean-Luc," said Marie. "He's taller. Maybe he can see over to the other side of the car. The two girls slid their way through the crowd. They reached Jean-Luc's side only after being squeezed in between what seemed like a thousand pairs of legs and half a million seat backs.

"Have you seen Grant anywhere?" asked Christina. "We can't find him, and I'm afraid he got left back at the station."

"No, he's not with me," replied Jean-Luc. "Don't worry," he advised, seeing the concern on Christina's face. "I am sure he is just hidden somewhere in this crowd."

As Jean-Luc finished his sentence, the train lurched to a halt, throwing everybody forward. The doors opened and there was a rush of people entering and exiting. At the far end of the car, there was a man with a guitar wedged in with the other passengers. As the train began to move, the man began to strum his guitar and sing a beautiful, sad melody in French. Christina was enchanted. At the end of his song, the passengers clapped and threw coins into his hat which lay on the seat beside him.

The train made another stop. All of the

people except the children left the car, and there were only a few waiting on the platform. Christina could now see the interior of the car clearly. Grant was nowhere to be found. Now she was genuinely worried. She went to tell Jean-Luc and Marie, but they were listening intently to the conversation of a man and a woman seated in front of them.

"Do you think it's true?" said Marie. "That would be so terrible!"

"What's wrong?" asked Christina. She hoped it wasn't about Grant.

"It's the windstorm," replied Marie. "That woman was saying that it is one of the worst Paris has ever experienced. The wind speeds are breaking all kinds of records. She mentioned something about the Eiffel Tower falling down!"

"That would be such a tragedy!" said Jean-Luc. "The *Tour* is our most famous monument!"

"Think of the danger too," added Marie, her eyes wide with concern. "That man is saying that it might just topple right over in a really strong gust of wind!"

"The *Tour* does sway in the wind," said Jean-Luc. "With the wind like it is today, it might fall down!"

The two French children sat morosely in silence. The prospect of losing their beloved tower was indeed a terrible thought. Christina, however, was concerned with something else: her missing brother. As she pondered, the train lurched to another halt. This was the third stop. Christina looked through the car's window and saw the sign on the white tile wall of the station. "*Solférino*," it read.

"This is our stop! Everybody off!" commanded Jean-Luc. Christina stepped apprehensively off the train, looking for Grant all the while.

Spooky Statues

"Where could he be?" wondered Christina out loud. "Grant? Grant, where are you?" she called, looking along the metro station's platform. Brother and sister had gotten separated on the train. Christina took a few steps towards the exit. Jean-Luc and Marie followed close behind.

"UUUUUURP!!" A huge belch sounded next to Christina. "EXCUSEM-WAH!" proclaimed a voice in a Southern drawl, a voice that was unmistakably Grant's. Christina turned to find her little brother standing next to her.

Christina grabbed Grant by the shoulders. "Where did you come from? I mean, where did you go? I mean, where have you been?" she exclaimed in confusion.

"I got on a different car, silly," said Grant. "It was too crowded in the first one. Don't tell me I had you worried."

"Of course you did!" said Christina. "What if we had lost you in Paris, and you not speaking a word of French!"

"I can say 'excuse me,'" smirked Grant.

"That's ok, we don't need another demonstration," said Christina. "Your first one was rude enough. But I have to say," she added, ruffling Grant's hair, "I've never been so glad to see you!"

The group made its way out of the *Métro* station onto the street and towards the imposing building of the Musée d'Orsay.

"I'm so glad we found you!" said Marie. "If you had gotten lost, it would be even more horrible than the *Tour* falling down!"

"What's this about a falling tour?" asked Grant. "I personally like to take my tours standing up, no tripping involved."

"No, it's the Eiffel Tower. It's in danger of falling over in this huge windstorm," explained Christina.

"We heard a woman talking about it on the *Métro*," said Jean-Luc.

"Eiffel Tower's falling down, falling down, falling down," sang Grant to the tune of "London Bridge."

"Please, don't joke about it," said Marie glumly.

"Here we are," said Jean-Luc. The group had arrived at the doors to the museum. "I'll go get tickets," he said, walking over towards the counter.

When he returned, four colorful tickets in hand, the children made their way into the museum, passing through the metal detectors carefully watched over by security guards. If I had all this precious artwork in *my* house, I'd have security guards and metal detectors too, thought Christina.

The kids made their way through the gates into the museum's main room. It had vast, soaring ceilings with huge, arched windows at one end. The floor was covered in a forest of beautiful statues and sculptures, some twice as tall as the admiring people that stood next to them. Bronze warriors and marble maidens watched over stone lions. The children wandered among the statues, taking in each detail with awe.

"I've never seen a room this big," said Christina.

"It used to be a train station," said Marie. "It was renovated and opened as a museum in 1986, I think."

Christina wandered into a side room off the main floor. The walls were covered in large canvases in ornate frames like the paintings in the Louvre, but these pictures had a different look. The faces and figures seemed softer and lighter. The subjects of the paintings seemed to be everyday people doing everyday things, not grand kings and emperors decked out in all their finery. Christina paused in front of a portrait of a young woman holding a water jug. Her face was so peaceful, with kind eyes and a gentle smile. She is almost more beautiful than the Mona Lisa, thought Christina.

There was a tug on her sleeve. She turned to find Marie standing next to her. "Let's go find the Van Gogh paintings like the one we saw on the clue," she said. Christina followed her over to a staircase where Jean-Luc and Grant were waiting. The group climbed the stairs to the third floor.

They wandered through a hallway lined on

both sides with small rooms. They paused in front of a dimly-lit doorway. Inside, they discovered glass cases filled with beautiful pastel drawings by the artist Edgar Degas. His favorite subject seemed to be ballerinas, as there were several pictures displaying dancers in motion with their frilly costumes outspread. They looked like they could jump and turn right off the paper, thought Christina. There was a plaque explaining that the light had to be kept dim in order to protect the fragile pastel drawings.

"Hey, Christina," whispered Grant. "It's so dark in here we could play hide and seek!" Christina grabbed the collar of his shirt. "No, sir, you're not going anywhere where I can't find you again! Just stay close, okay?"

"All right, all right," Grant replied. "Just trying to have a little fun!"

The kids moved down the hall in the midst of a fairly large crowd. They ended up in another large room lined with paintings. There was almost a solid wall of people in front of the paintings. Christina stood on her tiptoes but couldn't see a thing. She motioned to the others to join her, and they slowly edged their way to the front of the crowd. The paintings directly in front of them were created by the famous artist Vincent Van Gogh.

"Here we are," said Jean-Luc, digging in his pocket for the clue. "These are the paintings we want to see." He unfolded the slip of paper so they could see the tiny picture on it.

"Look, it's just ahead," said Christina. "Let's go this way. These paintings seem to be mostly landscapes."

The group squeezed its way over to another corner of the room. On the wall before them hung an impressive painting. It was a head of a man with a bright orange beard and piercing eyes. He had a sober expression on his face. The colors were mostly shades of blue, except for the vivid auburn color of the hair and beard. Christina noticed that the brushstrokes seemed to be straight lines radiating outward from the man's face. The plaque next to the painting read "Self-portrait."

Jean-Luc, Grant, and Marie wiggled in next to her. Jean-Luc held up the clue. The picture on it was an exact match to the portrait on the wall! "It's a perfect copy in **miniature**!" said Christina.

"Umm...now what?" asked Grant. "The clue

doesn't say what to do next. Maybe we should put our 'heads' together..." he smiled. "Get it?"

"This is not a time to joke, Grant," said Marie, downcast. "We have to figure out what to do next."

"Cheer up," said Jean-Luc. "Let's continue to look around. Maybe we will find something in another part of the museum.

Christina wasn't listening to their conversation. She had recognized a lady standing near the doorway at the far edge of the room. The woman looked familiar. She was wearing a long black coat. That's the woman from the bridge! We just keep on running into her, thought Christina. "I hope she's not following us," she murmured aloud. The woman watched the four kids with a menacing stare. "Let's get out of here," Christina said to her friends. "I get a creepy feeling from this place." As she turned to leave, she felt the steely eyes of Van Gogh's self-portrait riveted into the back of her head. *Was he watching the children too?*

* * *

Once the kids were back in the main part of the museum, Christina glanced over her shoulder to make sure the strange woman in black–or the ghost of Van Gogh!–wasn't following them. The kids searched among the statues, trying to find anything that would lead them onward on the trail of the mystery they were following. I wonder if we really *are* on the trail of the missing statue, thought Christina. It would be wonderful if we could catch the thief and return the statue to the museum. She fell into a daydream of rewards and glory. Maybe even the mayor of Paris or the president of France would come to thank her! She envisioned her picture on the front page of all the big newspapers and sumptuous banquets in her honor.

She was brought out of her reverie by Grant. "Do you *really* think the Eiffel Tower is going to fall down?" he questioned. "That's where we're supposed to eat dinner tonight."

"I hope not," Christina replied. She tried to hide her all-too-real concern. What if the tower collapsed while they were in the restaurant or on one of the elevators? She shuddered at the thought. She worried about Mimi and Papa and Cyril and Madame Dominique. What if they were already at the tip-top on the observation deck, looking out over the city? Could they feel the huge iron structure swaying in the blustering winds? Don't think like that, she told herself. It's probably impossible for something that sturdy to get blown over by the wind. But she already felt the doubt come creeping back into her mind. To distract herself, she continued her search for clues.

Jean-Luc called the rest of the kids over to join him. He stood next to a white marble statue of a woman. She was dressed in a flowing robe, the kind that women of ancient Rome wore. Her hair was long and curly, and it fell down over her shoulders almost to her waist. One arm was curved over her head, and the other was extended out in front of her. She leaned slightly forward, her knees bent and one foot placed to the side. She looked like she was dancing.

"*Regardez,*" said Jean-Luc, pointing. The others looked in the direction of the statue's outstretched arm. Something was resting in the palm of her hand! Christina reached out to take whatever it was. She hesitated as she felt the cold touch of the marble fingers. The creepy sensation gave her chills.

"I bet we found our next clue!" she exclaimed

triumphantly. But there was no time to celebrate. A guard had seen her touch the statue's hand, and he was striding angrily towards her. He doesn't look too pleased about my little handshake, she thought.

"Uh-oh, he saw you!" said Grant. "Let's make like a tree...and LEAVE!" he chuckled.

"No time for jokes now!" said Jean-Luc. The kids ran towards the exit. The guard, seeing the children dashing for the door, broke into a run himself. He was getting closer with every stride! Just in time, the children flew through the doorway out onto the street. The guard stood panting behind the glass, shaking his fist and muttering in frustration. Was he going to come after them? The group didn't stop to think. They continued running down the street for several blocks, never looking back once. Finally they ducked into an alleyway and listened for any angry footsteps coming behind them.

What the children didn't see was the guard pick up the phone and make a call. He rattled on in rapid French for at least two minutes, shaking his fist as he spoke. *But whom did he call?*

Ghoulish Gargoyles

"Whew! That was a narrow escape!" panted Christina. The others breathed a sigh of relief when they realized that the guard from the Musée d'Orsay was not following them.

"I'm glad he didn't catch up with us! We sure would have been in some big trouble," said Grant. He bent over to catch his breath.

"At least you got the clue without the guard noticing," said Jean-Luc.

"Let's look at it," said Marie. Christina took the slip of paper from her pocket and smoothed out the wrinkles. It had gotten squashed and crumpled in the rush to leave the museum. There was another short sentence written in

French. She handed it to Marie to read and translate once again.

"I guess you're the interpreter," joked Christina.

"That's what I want to do when I grow up!" said Marie. "I suppose this is good practice."

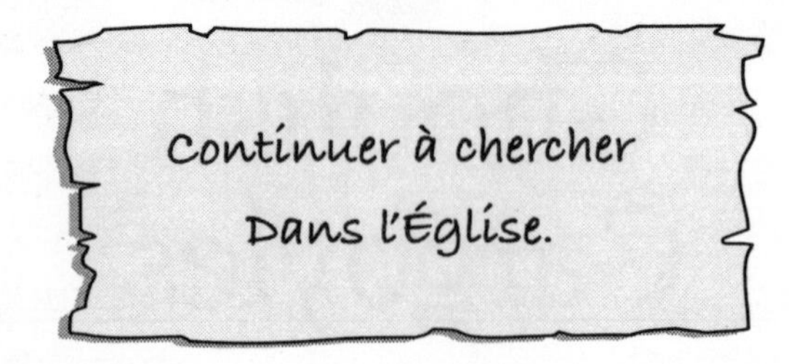

Marie paused for a moment to think before she gave the English meaning. "Continue to search in the church."

"Well, that one is easy enough," said Jean-Luc. "Everyone knows the most famous church in Paris...Notre Dame!"

"Ooooh, as in where the Hunchback lives?" asked Grant.

"That's right," said Jean-Luc. "That's the setting for the famous Victor Hugo novel."

"Don't they have gargles there?" asked Grant.

"Gargles? What does 'gargles' mean?" asked Marie. "I have never heard that English word before."

"You know, like you do with mouthwash," said Christina. She demonstrated by making bubbling noises in her throat. "But I think Grant means *gargoyles*," she added.

"Oh, I understand now," said Marie. "I have a new English word to use. And yes, there are the famous gargoyles at Notre Dame. They are quite creepy. They look like stone monsters!"

"Do you know what they were originally used for?" asked Jean-Luc.

"To scare annoying little brothers?" said Christina hopefully.

"They were rain gutters!" said Jean-Luc. "They were made so that the water would run off through their mouths."

"I bet it looks like they're spitting, like those fish we saw in the fountain at the Place de la Concorde," said Christina.

"Monster spit!" said Grant.

"Hush! That's disgusting!" admonished Christina in her "big sister" voice. But Grant didn't hear her. He was too busy creeping around, bent over with his arms extended and his hands curled like talons.

"I'm a gargoyle!" he said in his best spooky voice. The group laughed.

"Well come on, Gargle the Gargoyle," joked Christina. "Let's head over to Notre Dame." To Jean-Luc and Marie she said, "Lead the way!"

* * *

The kids walked in single file down the bustling streets. Jean-Luc led the way. Christina followed behind, taking in all the sights and sounds that she could. Despite the season, the air was chilly and more and more clouds were building in the sky. The strong wind continued to blow in large gusts, whipping the children's hair around. The sounds of cars rushing by, horns beeping, and faint music drifting from the street side shops swirled into Christina's ears.

Suddenly, Jean-Luc stopped short. Christina almost ran into him. *I'd better pay attention,* she thought as she looked up to see why they had stopped. A large roadblock diverted traffic onto a side street. The kids' way was barred. A huge crowd of people stood along the roadblock. Some were waving flags and cheering.

"What's the deal? Is there construction?" asked Grant. "I never heard of people cheering for construction workers. Maybe there's food," he sighed. "I'm getting hungry."

Marie's eyes widened as she answered. "It's the Tour de France!" she exclaimed.

"*The* Tour de France? The famous bicycle race? Right here?" Christina questioned incredulously.

"Yes, I forgot!" said Jean-Luc. "They must be passing though Paris today!" Christina could sense the excitement in his voice.

"Let's wait a moment and see if we can see anything," suggested Marie.

Christina couldn't believe that she might get to witness a small segment of the long, grueling bicycle race that took its participants all over France. The kids edged in closer to the roadblock to get a better view. The people standing further down the way started to cheer.

"Here they come!" said Jean-Luc. He could see best because he was the tallest. *Whoosh!* What seemed like a large blur composed of helmets and wheels whizzed by the children. As the blur passed down the avenue into the distance, Christina could pick out the individual riders. The leader, wearing a bright yellow biking shirt, was far ahead of the pack.

"The guy in front is dressed like a

highlighter!" crowed Grant.

"That's the famous yellow jersey," explained Jean-Luc. "It is worn by the leader. At the end of the race, the winner gets to keep it.

"I think it would make a great Halloween costume," said Grant. "Plus, I could ride my bike around the neighborhood." Grant's eyes got big. " Think how much more candy I could get!" he exclaimed.

Halloween ... bats ... ghosts ... Christina's mind wandered at the mention of the spooky holiday. *Snap out of it,* she told herself. *There's nothing to be afraid of.* Still, she felt an uneasy feeling creeping over her. *Who knew what they would find as they continued their search for the missing statue? And what about the Eiffel Tower? Is it still in danger from this windstorm,* she wondered?

Jean-Luc interrupted her gloomy train of thought. "We have to find another way to get to the church since this street is blocked," he said. He paused to think for a minute, and then confidently struck out in a different direction, motioning for the others to follow him.

* * *

The soaring outline of Notre Dame's two bell towers dominated the small square in front of the famous church. To Christina's surprise, it was relatively empty. Everyone must be watching the bike race, she thought. She gazed up at the church's entrance. Two smaller doors flanked the large one in the center of the building. Stone arches carved with rows of statues rose gracefully over each doorway. Christina moved in closer to get a better look. She gazed up into the statues' faces. They seemed to be staring blankly out into space. Many of them were dressed in long robes and sandals, and they had crowns on their heads. Their peaceful expressions and serene hand gestures gave Christina a calm feeling.

"Those are statues of saints," said Marie. She pointed toward the arches. "Each arch tells a story. If we get closer, you can see."

"It is a shame, though," interjected Jean-Luc. "A lot of the statues have been broken over time." Christina looked closely. She could see that some of the statues were missing pieces of their crowns and robes, hands, feet, and even...*heads*. She gasped. There I go again, she thought. I need to stop thinking about creepy things. She felt Marie grab her by the hand.

"Let's go inside," she said. Jean-Luc pulled open the large, squeaky wooden door. A sign on the wall in several languages admonished visitors to please remain quiet. The children filed in slowly. The air inside the dark church was cool. The thick, gray stone walls supported a soaring arched ceiling. Beautiful stained glass windows illuminated the rows and rows of wooden pews. Thousands of tiny candles on racks flickered like faraway stars.

"Why don't we spread out and search for clues," suggested Christina. "Jean-Luc, you take the left side. Grant, you take the right. Marie, why don't you go search the front, and I'll take the back. When we're done, let's meet back here to climb up into the bell towers."

"Sounds like a good plan," said Grant. For once, he was too awestruck by the beautiful building to argue with his big sis. The kids split up to examine the huge sanctuary. Christina walked slowly along the back wall of the church. She noticed a plaque on the wall with writing in what looked like French, Spanish, German, Italian, and Japanese. She looked down to the English section. It told a bit about the history of the church.

"Look at this," Christina motioned to Grant. "Construction on this church began in 1163 and wasn't completed until 1345." Grant did a quick math calculation in his head. "Why did it take almost 200 years?" he asked. "Well, you must remember," said Jean-Luc, "they did not have machines to help them build back then. People did all the work!"

"That sure gives a new meaning to the word 'manpower,'" said Christina.

Christina was amazed to think she was walking on such an ancient floor. She imagined all the other people that had walked on this floor: chanting monks, devoted pilgrims, and thousands and thousands of tourists like her. She turned around and looked across the sanctuary to the large stained glass rose window. Faint sunlight filtered through its many-colored circular shape. It was surrounded by more stained glass shapes depicting biblical stories and French history.

I'd better get back to searching, she thought. She paced around the back of the church, making sure to look in all of the nooks and crannies that she could find. She was peering into a particularly dark, dusty corner when she felt a poke in her ribs. "Yikes!" she exclaimed with a jump.

"Gotcha!" said Grant. "You're too easy to scare." Now is *not* the time, she thought. Marie and Jean-Luc came tiptoeing up next to them.

"Did anybody find anything?" asked Christina.

"Nothing," said Jean-Luc.

"Nothing," said Marie.

"Nothing," said Grant.

"Hmm. I hope we're not in the wrong place," said Christina.

"Don't give up yet," said Marie. "Let's go search in the bell towers."

The kids made their way out to the staircase. Christina sighed with disappointment. A velvet rope barred the entrance. Off limits!

"What should we do?" she asked, discouraged.

"Well..." said Jean-Luc. "Look," he said, pointing. No guards were in sight. There were only a few other tourists milling around silently and respectfully. In the gift shop window, a gray-haired clerk dozed as he tried to read the newspaper. *He* certainly wasn't paying attention to a few kids creeping around!

"Do you mean...*sneak up there*?" whispered Christina incredulously.

"Very quietly," said Jean-Luc. "I hate to think what kind of trouble we'd be in if we got caught!"

"Well, let's go," said Christina. "But let's make it quick!"

The kids slipped one by one under the velvet cord. They tiptoed as quietly as possible up the creaky old staircase. After what seemed like half an hour of climbing, they finally reached the top.

"Whew! I feel like a mountain climber!" Grant crowed.

"Shh!" said Christina. "Let's look around and then get OUT of here!" The group fanned out to continue the search.

After a moment, Jean-Luc motioned them over to a small door. "Let's see where it leads," he murmured. I don't like the looks of this, thought Christina. The door opened with a whoosh of cold air. It led to the rooftop! The children stepped out into the chilly wind. Grant gulped a big gulp.

"I hope we don't get blown over the edge," he said, grabbing Christina's arm.

"Don't look down, just look up," advised Marie. Christina tilted her head back and squinted at the sky. Gray clouds swirled and small flashes of lightning flickered in the distance. Looking at the moving clouds gave her a dizzy feeling. She instinctively backed up right into a...

"EEK!" she squealed in alarm. She had backed into something sharp! She rubbed her back where she had gotten a vicious poke. She whirled around to face whatever it was. "EEK!" she cried again. She was face-to-face with a terrible gray monster!

"It's all right!" said Marie, rushing to her side. "It's just one of the gargoyles we were talking about! Relax!"

Christina stepped back to examine her stony attacker. It was a monster indeed! It looked like a griffin, with a lion's body and a bird's head. Large, feathery wings curved up above its back. It had sharp talons on its front feet. That must be what I ran into, thought Christina.

"Prrr! Prrr!" A familiar coo reached her ears as a pigeon perched on the gargoyle's head. He cocked his head and bobbed back and forth a few times. "Prrr! Prrr!" he repeated.

"You look familiar," muttered Christina. "Haven't we met before?" She scrutinized the pigeon's markings. It can't be the same pigeon I saw on the Arc de Triomphe, she thought. There must be millions and millions of pigeons in Paris. I'm letting my imagination get away with me. Still, the pigeon looked at her with his little beady eyes as if he knew something. "Weird bird," she muttered.

"Yeah, it *is* weird-looking," agreed Grant, pointing to the gargoyle. "I've never seen a bird with a lion's tail!" The pigeon got spooked at Grant's voice and sudden movements. He flapped his wings and flew off directly over their heads.

Plop!

"GROSS!" cried Grant in disgust. "He pooped on my head!"

"Oh no!" said Christina. "That's the most disgusting thing ever!"

"Here, I have some tissues," offered Marie. Christina tried to wipe the mess out of Grant's hair, but he was squealing and squirming too much for her to do any good.

"You'll just have to wait until you can take a bath," she said.

"That's one bath I won't object to," said Grant. "This is SOOO GRROOOOSSSS– and it smells horrible!"

During the commotion over the pigeon poop, Jean-Luc had been staring intently at the griffin gargoyle. He reached up and took something out of its wicked-looking gray stone beak. "Look, everybody!" he said. "I think I found the clue!"

"*Mais non! Mais non*!" cried an angry female voice.

"W-w-what was that?" asked a terrified Christina.

"RUN!!" was the last thing she heard as she raced down the stairs.

Sinister Snails

The kids' shoes made loud clattering noises on the stone staircase. "Keep going!" shouted Jean-Luc as they reached the bottom. They sped through the back of the church. A guard, drawn by the racket in the stairwell, spotted the kids and started yelling in French. He pursued them to the big wooden door. Christina pushed it open, and the others rushed through it. She checked behind her to see if the shadowy owner of the angry voice from the rooftop was following them. Nobody in sight.

What the children didn't see was the guard shake his head and walk back to his station. He picked up the phone to make a call. He looked out the window as he spoke, craning his neck like he was searching for someone or something.

He finally hung up the phone and sat down in his black leather chair. *But whom did he call?*

* * *

Once they were out on the street, the kids found a big bench and crouched down behind it. "We just made it!" panted Marie.

Christina looked around cautiously for any followers. "I think we're safe now," she said.

"Boy, whoever was up on the roof back there sure was mad that we found that clue in the gargoyle's mouth!" said Grant.

"You can say that again," said Christina. "It seems like she was also looking for the clue. Otherwise, what would she have been doing sneaking around up on the roof?"

"And why would she have been so angry when we found this clue–or whatever it's supposed to be?" added Marie.

"Maybe it was just another guard who was telling us not to touch the gargoyles," proposed Jean-Luc. "It might not have anything to do with this so-called clue."

Christina had to admit that he had a point. She was thoroughly confused. No matter who that person on the roof was or what they were doing up there, Christina still got the feeling that they were mixed up in something they had no business being mixed up in!

"Let's see what this clue says," she said. The others gathered around to look. This time, it was another picture–no writing.

"Okay, that's just creepy," said Grant, looking at the sinister image. A skull and crossbones stared out from the paper. "It looks like a Jolly Roger flag from a pirate ship!" he said.

"True," said Christina in agreement. "Could this have anything to do with ships or boats or the sea...or the river?" she asked.

"I think I know what it means," said Jean-Luc, deep in thought. "Bones...a skull and bones," he muttered. "Yes, I think that is it."

"I don't like the sound of this," said Christina.

"Do you mean the catacombs?" asked Marie.

"You guessed it!" said Jean-Luc. "Where else in Paris do they keep bones?"

"What are catacombs?" asked Grant. "Is that like honeycombs?"

"Umm, not quite," said Christina. She didn't like where this conversation was going at all! "Catacombs are sort of like an underground graveyard," she explained.

"It's like a giant maze underground," added Marie.

"That must be what this clue means," said Jean-Luc.

"But what about the other graveyards, like the Cimetière du Père Lachaise?" asked Marie.

"It could be talking about that," replied Jean-Luc. "But the catacombs are full of bones."

"No more bones!" cried Grant. "The only bones I'm interested in right now are chicken bones...or turkey bones." He rubbed his growling tummy.

"Good idea!" said Christina. "Why don't we stop for a snack."

"That sounds good to me," said Marie. "At least we can get out of this chilly wind," she added, shivering.

Ring! Ring! Jean-Luc grabbed for the cell

phone that was clipped to his belt. "*Âllo?*" he said. Christina watched as Jean-Luc spoke. She had asked for a cell phone for Christmas. It would be just for emergencies, she had told her mother. It was a good thing Jean-Luc had one today, she thought, in case I need to call Mimi.

"It must be our parents," whispered Marie.

After a short conversation in French, Jean-Luc flipped his phone closed. "It was *Mama* and *Papa*," he said. "They told us to be extra careful–there is a big thunderstorm forecast for this evening!"

"I can believe that," said Grant, glancing up at the sky. It was dark gray and menacing.

"Let's get inside!" said Christina.

"How about this café?" asked Marie.

"Looks good to me," said Grant. "I don't care *where* it is as long as they serve food!"

The kids crossed the street and opened the door of the tiny café. The door chimes jingled. A waiter was gathering up the sidewalk tables and chairs and carrying them inside. He smiled at the children from under his burden of stacked-up chairs. The strong wind whipped his long white apron.

The café was almost vacant. The waiter

gestured, indicating that the kids could sit anywhere they wanted. They claimed a table by the window. Christina felt so grown-up. Here I am wandering around Paris, eating in a café with my two French pen pals. "I'll have to tell Mimi about this place!" she said to the others.

"Tell me what to order," said Grant, who was preoccupied with the delicious smell coming from the kitchen. "How about some more crêpes?"

"We have a surprise for you," said Jean-Luc. He winked mischievously. He whispered something to the waiter, who laughed and dashed off to the kitchen.

"Uh-oh," said Christina. "I hope we're going to like this!" she said.

"Don't worry," said Jean-Luc. "You're about to sample one of the famous French specialties."

The waiter returned with their drinks. He set down four tall, frosty glasses of what looked like water. When Christina picked up her glass, she noticed tiny, fizzy bubbles floating around in the liquid. It smelled sweet.

"This is a *limonade,*" said Marie.

"Lemonade?" asked Grant.

"Well, sort of," said Marie. "It's lemon-flavored and delicious."

"Wow, this is great!" exclaimed Christina. "It does taste just like lemonade, only fizzy!" She quickly gulped down the rest. "How do you say 'More drink, please?'" she asked with a laugh. She was interrupted by the waiter's return.

"*Voilà*!" he said as he placed down their plates.

"What in the world?" said Grant.

Christina studied her dish. It had six little hollows, each holding...a snail shell! She had always heard that snails were a great delicacy in France, but here she was, face-to-face with six real ones on her plate!

"Oh no!" she howled. "I really don't think I can eat this!"

Grant's blue eyes widened. "Are you serious?" he asked. "The last time I saw a snail it was crawling around in Mimi's garden. And it left this slimy stuff behind it as it moved! There's no way I'm eating that!"

"Just try them," said Jean-Luc. "You don't have to eat them if you hate them."

"Come on, just one bite," pled Marie.

Christina watched her French friends hungrily attack the snails. They used special tongs to hold the shell and a tiny fork to pick out the meat. The meat itself was gray and covered in some kind of leafy green stuff.

"Okay, here goes nothing," said Christina as she gingerly picked up a shell. She had a little trouble with the tongs, but she finally got a hold of a piece of meat. "Watch out!" cried Grant. "I think it's moving!"

"Cut it out, Grant," Christina said. She took a deep breath. Closing her eyes, she slowly put it in her mouth and chewed. She was pleasantly surprised! The snail, which she had expected to taste revolting, actually had a buttery, spicy flavor. "This is *good*!" she exclaimed in disbelief.

"See? I knew you would like it!" said Marie.

"Try yours, Grant," urged Christina, eagerly attacking her second snail.

"Well, I guess I can pretend that I've been lost in the woods and I haven't eaten for three days," Grant said with a frown on his face. He sniffed the snails on his plate and looked at his sister. "Go ahead, Grant," Christina urged. "You used to eat bugs when you were a baby!"

Grant took a tiny taste of a snail. His head jerked up in surprise. "Wow!" he exclaimed. "It's a little chewy, but I like it!"

Marie and Jean-Luc were obviously delighted that their American friends liked the gourmet French treat. "Now you can tell all your friends that you ate *snails*!" said Jean-Luc.

"Mom will never believe this!" said Grant.

"Yeah, especially since she has such a hard time getting you to eat your broccoli," teased Christina.

The kids laughed. Christina concentrated on the delicious morsels in front of her. Before she knew it, she had eaten all her snails! "That was a good snack even if it was a little unusual," she admitted.

"That's one of the fun things about traveling," said Marie. "I love to meet new people and try new foods."

"Back on task now," said Christina, as they paid the waiter for their food. "I suppose we have to go to the catacombs now."

"I don't like the sound of this," said Grant, who looked more than a little nervous. "There are probably skulls down there ... you know ... *heads*!"

"Come on," said Jean-Luc. "We just have to find that statue!"

A Chilling Chase

Outside the café, the wind was blowing and the sky looked as if it would start to rain any minute. The kids huddled together on the street corner. Christina felt like she was about to be blown over by the huge gusts. Lightning flickered on the horizon.

"I've never seen it this windy before," said Marie. "What is happening to the Eiffel Tower right now?"

"Don't worry. I'm sure this storm will pass through quickly." Christina tried to sound reassuring, but this looked like it was going to be worse than any thunderstorm she had ever seen. She worried that Mimi and Papa would be watching for them, but she hated to abandon their search.

"Ok, we need to go this way," said Jean-Luc, pointing down the street. "We'll have to take the *Métro* again. That will save us a lot of time."

"Yeah, we can't be late for dinner!" said Christina. "Mimi would kill us!"

"And don't forget, we have to go by our apartment and change," added Marie.

"AND wash this pigeon poop out of my hair!" said Grant miserably.

"Oh, you'll live for now," said Christina.

"Turn left here," said Jean-Luc. He was looking at a small object he held in his hand.

"Is that your cell phone?" asked Christina.

"No, this is a handheld computer," he said, obviously proud to show it off. "My parents gave it to me as a birthday present."

"What does it do?" asked a curious Grant.

"All kinds of things," said Jean-Luc. "It has a calendar and an address book. You can even play games or log onto the internet!"

"Whoa, that's awesome!" said Grant. "I want one!"

"I'm looking at the city map now to find the nearest *Métro* station," said Jean-Luc.

The kids continued to plod ahead. Christina was feeling a little tired. This has been a crazy day so far, she said to herself. I just hope it doesn't get any crazier! She looked around, taking in the sights and sounds. People seemed like they were in a big hurry to get somewhere. They probably want to get inside before the storm starts, thought Christina.

The traffic light ahead turned red. The cars on the street beside the children slowed to a halt. There was a big, shiny black car right next to the children. Christina examined it. Its windows were tinted so she couldn't see inside. One of the windows rolled down about halfway. A woman's face peered out.

"That's her!" Christina said in a low voice, nudging Marie.

"That's who?" asked Marie.

"The woman who's been following us!" explained Christina.

"Someone's been following us?" said Marie. "I haven't noticed anyone."

"Well, I'm not exactly sure that she's following us," explained Christina. "But I have seen her several times today," she asserted. "What are the odds of that?"

"Jean-Luc, do you know that woman?" Marie asked her brother, pointing him in the direction of the black car.

He studied the black-haired woman's face. She was wearing dark sunglasses that made it impossible to tell where she was looking, but she seemed to be staring in the children's direction. The traffic light changed to green, and the cars pulled away from the intersection. The woman was gone.

"No, I have never seen her before," said Jean-Luc. "You think she's following us?" he asked Christina.

"I think she might be," said Christina. "So far today I've seen her in quite a few places. I just don't think that running into her that many times could be a coincidence."

"Oh boy, I hope she's not following us," said Grant. "What would she want with us?"

Christina thought for a moment. Maybe the kids had stumbled upon something, and the woman was trying to prevent them from getting further involved. Oh no, thought Christina. Who knows what we've gotten ourselves into?

"I guess we didn't keep our promise to stay 'mystery-free' on this trip," she said to Grant.

"It's too bad, huh?" he said. "We could have had a nice, peaceful tour of Paris, but we're headed to a graveyard instead!" he exclaimed woefully.

Up ahead was a sign that said "*Métro*."

"Here we go!" said Jean-Luc, heading down the stairway. The others followed. He paused to look at the map on the wall. "Okay," he said. "We have to be extra careful and stick close together. We'll have to change trains four times. Everybody ready?" he asked.

"Yes!" the other three said in unison. This time, the kids bought their tickets from an automatic vending machine. They stamped them in the machine and headed down a set of staircases to the train platform. They arrived just as the train was pulling into the station.

"Two stops on this train," said Jean-Luc.

"Stick with me, Grant," admonished Christina. "We can't have you getting separated again."

"Yes, Big Sister," he replied, tilting his head and giving Christina an angelic smile.

The train doors clicked shut, and Christina held onto the seat in front of her as the train lurched forward into motion. After a few moments of bumpy riding, they arrived in a second station that looked identical to the first, right down to the white brick walls.

"Did we even go anywhere?" joked Grant.

"One more stop, then we have to switch trains," Jean-Luc reminded everyone.

At the next station, the kids exited the car and followed Jean-Luc and Marie up and down some staircases and through two long hallways until they came to another platform. They waited impatiently for the train. After a few minutes, one pulled into the station. The doors opened, but very few people exited. The kids scrambled on board. To their surprise, the car was almost empty!

"We finally get to sit down!" said Christina, choosing a spot near the door. Marie plopped down next to her, while Grant ran around and around the pole in the back of the car.

"It's unusual for a car to be this empty," said Marie suspiciously.

"I guess we're not going to a very popular destination," said Christina, trying to lighten up the situation. "At least we have the entire car to...ourselves," her speech trailed off as she noticed the only other passenger.

The woman in black was sitting in the very corner of the car! She sat very straight, a big black bag resting on her knees. She still wore her sunglasses, even on the underground *Métro*. She seemed to be unaware of the children's presence.

"Grant, come here!" said Christina. Marie motioned for Jean-Luc to come sit down beside them. The kids gathered together in a huddle.

"Okay, now I'm almost one hundred percent sure that she's following us," whispered Christina. "This can't be a coincidence!"

"You are right," agreed Jean-Luc.

"But what does she want from us?" asked Marie. "We haven't done anything."

"Maybe she knows something about this mysterious missing statue," Christina speculated. "Could it be that she's trying to stop us from finding it?" she asked. "It's a possibility," said Jean-Luc. "But I think we should not let our imaginations get away from us."

The train slowed as it approached the next stop. "We get off here," said Marie. The kids made their way toward the door. So did the strange woman in black! "See!" hissed Christina in a whisper. "She *is* following us!"

"Get ready to run!" said Grant as the doors

sprang open. The four kids bolted out the door and ran up the staircase. Jean-Luc took the lead. Christina glanced back over her shoulder. Her worst fears were confirmed. The strange woman was running after them! At least she can't run too fast in high heels, thought Christina.

Jean-Luc took a sharp left turn into another tunnel, then a quick right into still another one. Christina felt like she was in some sort of underground hamster maze. "Almost there!" said Jean-Luc as they sprinted up a staircase. They could hear the woman's high heels behind them. Thankfully, there was a large crowd at the top of the stairs. The kids blended in quickly. Christina turned around carefully. The woman was standing at the far end of the hallway, looking around with a puzzled expression.

"I don't think she sees us!" she whispered to the others.

"Whew!" sighed Marie. "That was close!"

Jean-Luc pointed them toward the correct platform. "Here's our next train," he said. Christina was a little shaken up by the chase. Hopefully they had lost the woman in the crowd. *But will they have company on this train too?*

Death's Domain

After the wild chase through the tunnels of the *Métro* and two more nervous train rides, the kids finally arrived at the entrance to the catacombs. They stood outside the building and peered in through the glass door. There were two guards behind the counter, apparently deeply involved in a conversation. Christina pushed open the door quietly. "Let's try to sneak past them," she whispered.

The group silently filed in one by one, keeping a cautious eye on the guards the whole time. The two men behind the counter didn't once look in their direction. "So far, so good," Christina whispered with a sigh of relief. She made her way over to a stairwell in the corner of the room, where a sign with an arrow stood on a pole. "I guess that's where the tour starts," she murmured. She ushered the others over to where she was standing.

"I'm not so sure I want to do this," whispered Grant. "Just thinking about it is giving me the creeps!"

"We'll be fine," reassured Christina. She really hoped they would. Although she would never admit it to Grant, she was feeling a little spooked herself. She and Grant had been in plenty of creepy situations before, but never in one like this! *There are no such things as ghosts,* she repeated to herself over and over again. *There are no such things as ghosts.*

"Hurry," whispered Jean-Luc. He pointed to the guards, who were talking to a visitor who had just come in the door. The kids quietly tiptoed down into the stairwell. This isn't getting off to a very good start, thought Christina, as the group slowly made their descent. The spiral staircase itself was old and dingy, with only a thick, worn rope in place of a handrail. Most of the fluorescent lights overhead were burned out, and the bulbs that remained flickered ominously. We should have brought flashlights, she thought.

A musty smell and a cold, damp feeling in the

air told the children that they were near the end of the staircase. As they stepped off the last stair onto the uneven stone floor, Christina noticed an inscription above the archway that led into the catacombs themselves. "What does that say?" she whispered to Jean-Luc.

"Stop! This is the empire of Death!" he read in a low voice. The words sent chills down Christina's spine. No wonder she felt as if they were trespassing. Here they were in Death's own domain–without permission! She was startled by a jab in her ribs. Grant looked up at her anxiously.

"I think I heard something," he murmured nervously. "Listen!" *Drip. Drip. Splash. Drip.* Christina heard a sound like a leaky faucet. Drops of water seemed to be falling into a puddle somewhere.

"What's that dripping noise?" she asked Marie.

"It's from the dampness in here," Marie responded. "There are underground water sources surrounding the catacombs, and they leak through the stone into the underground. Some areas have had to be closed because they become unsafe or flooded."

Oh great, thought Christina. Not only are we in a massive underground graveyard, we're in an underground graveyard that might flood!

Jean-Luc slowly led the group into the passageway ahead. It seemed to be a narrow hallway made out of stone. As they moved away from the stairwell, the light grew dimmer and dimmer until they could not see. "What do we do now?" said Marie. "We can't go any further without light."

Click! "AHHH!" Everyone jumped in fright. A floating head appeared in front of them, its eyes illuminated by a ghostly light.

"GRANT!" said Christina in frustration. "You scared us all half to death!"

"But I do have a flashlight!" he said with a giggle, enjoying the trick he had just played on the others. He showed them his blue pocket flashlight, complete with a key ring on one end of it. "Thank goodness I changed the batteries before this trip," he said.

"Just don't pull any more stunts like that," warned Christina. "If you do, you might *accidentally* get left behind in this creepy place," she said.

"Ok, I promise!" said Grant, shuddering at

the prospect of being alone in the catacombs.

"We should be quiet," reminded Jean-Luc. "We don't want the guards upstairs to hear us."

The group fell silent as they slowly moved forward. They came to the end of the narrow stone hallway. It opened into a large, low-ceilinged room. Grant shone his flashlight around. The beam flickered eerily off the walls. "Those aren't what I think they are...are they?" asked Christina.

"Yes, I am afraid they are," said Jean-Luc. Christina gasped.

The walls weren't really walls at all. They were stacks upon stacks upon stacks of bones! Some were long, skinny bones stacked together like logs in a woodpile. Other parts of the walls were skulls piled on top of each other in rows and columns. Still other walls were more stacks of the long, skinny bones interspersed with skulls at certain points to form a macabre pattern.

"This certainly is gruesome!" said Christina.

"It is sad," said Marie. "Most of the remains come from a cemetery near here called Les Halles. That graveyard was getting too crowded and dirty, so the city **excavated** it and moved all the bones here in 1786."

"That's awful!" said Christina. "All those poor, poor people." She gazed around the room at the patterns formed by the bones. There must be two hundred skulls in this room alone, she thought. It was hard to imagine the countless number of people who had been buried in one graveyard only to be moved here long after their deaths.

Grant and Marie stared at the walls, transfixed by all the bones. Each took slow, baby steps backward to take it all in. *Wham*! They backed right into each other. Marie screamed. Then Grant screamed louder.

"Oh, Grant! You scared me!" she gasped. "You scared me, too," Grant replied. "This is the creepiest place I've ever been in!" All four kids burst into nervous laughter.

"Okay, everyone," said Christina, "let's keep moving. The sooner we get out of here, the better!"

They pressed forward, passing through similar rooms and more stone passageways. The floor was uneven and slippery. Water dripped steadily from above, sometimes hitting the children on their heads. "I'm getting a free shower!" said Grant. "Bird poop, be gone!"

The group stopped in one room to admire the patterns made by the stacks of bones. Christina saw the outline of a heart made of skulls. On the opposite wall was a cross also made of skulls. Below it, there was a stone plaque with chiseled writing. Christina could barely decipher the worn letters. She guessed that the words were written in Latin.

Grant peered closely at one particular skull on the wall. "I think I might have found something," he said. The others clustered around him to look. He aimed the flashlight at the skull. There was something white in its mouth. Christina gritted her teeth and reached in and pulled it out. It was a piece of paper. Another clue!

Before she could stop to read it, Marie tugged her arm. "I think we should hurry!" she said. "I hear someone coming!" Indeed, Christina heard the sound of footsteps coming toward them. The children rushed ahead as quietly as possible, stopping every few minutes to listen for the footsteps. They were steadily coming closer.

In her hurry, Christina failed to notice a large puddle. She slipped and fell smack down in the middle of it on her bottom! "Oh no!" she cried. "I'm covered in disgusting water! Who knows what's been in this water!"

"No time right now! We'll dry you off when we get outside," said Jean-Luc, giving her a helping hand up. They continued to press forward.

The group finally reached another staircase. They frantically climbed, not caring how much noise they made. Their biggest concern was getting away from their mysterious follower! A light glowed faintly at the top of the stairs. As they mounted the last steps, a guard's face came into view. Uh-oh, we're in trouble now, thought Christina. *They've found us!*

Lost Luggage

To everyone's pleasant surprise, the guard smiled kindly. "Did you enjoy your visit?" he asked in broken English. "I hope it was not too scary down there."

"Oh, uh, not at all," stammered Grant, still shaken by the prospect of getting caught sneaking around where he wasn't allowed.

"It was an interesting tour," said Christina. "Thank you very much. But how did you know to speak English to us? Is it that easy to tell we are Americans?" she questioned.

"I can always tell," said the guard with a wink. "Besides, I heard you down there speaking in English. I sent my coworker down to make sure that you were safe."

So that's who was following us, thought

Christina. At least we aren't in trouble.

"You must have fallen into a puddle," he said, indicating Christina's soaking wet skirt. She looked down. She was dripping brownish water all over the floor! "Let me get you a towel," said the guard.

"Thank you!" she said gratefully. "And sorry about the mess."

"No trouble at all," said the guard, handing her a clean, white towel. She scrubbed off her skirt as best as she could. I'm covered in slop, and Grant's got pigeon poop in his hair, she thought. What a sight we must be! She handed the towel back to the kindly guard.

"Thank you again for your help," she said.

"It is my pleasure," said the guard. "*Bonne journée*, or as you say, have a nice day!"

What the children didn't see was the guard cross his arms and walk quickly back inside. He dialed his phone and tapped his foot as he waited for someone to answer. His words were sharp and to the point. *But whom did he call?*

* * *

"Wow, we were sure lucky that time!" said

Grant as they stepped outside. "I'm glad that guard was such a nice guy."

"Thank goodness!" said Marie. "We would have been in some big trouble if he hadn't been so kind."

"So you found another clue?" Jean-Luc asked Christina.

"I sure did," she said proudly. "I just hope I didn't get it too wet when I fell into the puddle." She took the piece of paper and handed it to Marie. "Here you go, Ms. Interpreter," she said with a smile.

"Let's see," said Marie. She scrutinized the small scrap of white paper. "It says here that...Well, wait, it doesn't say anything!" she said in surprise.

"You mean it's blank?" asked Jean-Luc incredulously.

"Completely blank," said Marie.

Christina felt bummed out. "I guess I mistook a plain ol' scrap of paper for one of our so-called 'clues,'" she said dejectedly.

Just then, rain started to fall from the blackened sky. Wind gusts blew the big drops into the kids' faces. They moved underneath a nearby storefront awning to avoid getting soaked.

"Well, I got it wet after all," said Christina, holding up the sad-looking scrap of paper. A few raindrops had fallen on it, making it soggy.

"Wait a minute, may I see it?" asked Jean-Luc. Christina handed him the paper. He studied it for a moment. "I think you may have found the clue after all!" he said in amazement. "Look at this!"

The others took a look at the clue. Something dark was beginning to appear on the white paper's surface. "I think it's a written in a special kind of ink," said Jean-Luc. "One that has to get wet before it will show up on paper."

"I think you're right," said Christina. A shape was slowly beginning to materialize on the white paper.

"Cool!" said Grant. "It's just like the invisible ink that came with my spy kit! You write a message on a special kind of paper with invisible ink, then you dip it in water to reveal the message!"

"Exactly like that," agreed Christina.

"But it did make my handwriting look really bad because I couldn't see what I was writing!" said Grant. Everybody laughed.

The black blob had finally materialized

onto the paper. "Now that makes some sense!" said Jean-Luc.

Christina gazed at the paper. On it stood a miniature sketch of the Eiffel Tower with an arrow pointing to the very tip-top!

"That's the easiest clue yet!" said Marie. "We just have to go to the top of the *Tour Eiffel*!"

A sudden gust of wind snatched the clue out of Jean-Luc's hand. He chased after it for a few feet, but the wind blew it out of his reach. "I'm sorry I lost it," he said.

"It's okay," said Christina. "At least we got to see what was on it."

She hoped that it wasn't a bad omen. She recalled the rumors she and the other kids had heard about the Eiffel Tower being blown over by a tremendous wind. All kinds of questions rose up in her mind. What exactly are they chasing? Is it the statue missing from the Louvre? Who is this strange woman that seems to be following them? And most importantly, is the Tower itself in danger? She sincerely hoped that the people behind all these clues didn't have some kind of plan to bring down the tower.

Bong! Bong! Bong! Bong! Bong! Bong! The clock of a nearby church struck six o'clock with thunderous chimes, startling Christina out of her deep thought. Thunder rumbled in the distance as if in answer to the clock's magnificent chimes.

"Uh-oh!" said Grant. "We're supposed to be at that fancy-schmancy restaurant at seven o'clock! If we don't get a move on, we'll be late!"

"And if we're late..." said Christina.

"We're dead!" the whole group said in unison.

"We'll be skullbones in the catacombs," Grant said, pleased with his rhyme.

"Here's what we need to do," said Jean-Luc. "We'll take the *Métro* to our apartment, get cleaned up and ready to go, then take a cab to the Eiffel Tower to meet our parents and your grandparents."

"That would be the quickest way of doing things," said Marie.

"I don't know what we would have done without you here to plan everything and find our way around!" Christina said appreciatively to Jean-Luc.

"*Ce n'est rien,*" said Jean-Luc.

"Huh?" asked Grant. How can you ever learn all these French words, he thought.

"Oh, I meant that it was no trouble at all," said Jean-Luc. "Now, let's head home!"

* * *

The kids arrived at Jean-Luc and Marie's apartment just as the clock was striking six-fifteen. Marie unlocked the big wooden door and invited Grant and Christina to step inside. Christina was awestruck by the grandeur of the place. "I want to live here!" she said in amazement.

The living room of the apartment was long and spacious. It had a high ceiling with a large crystal chandelier hanging from it. The walls were covered in rich red wallpaper that looked almost velvety. The furniture was covered in shiny gold brocade fabric. Brocade is fabric with a raised pattern on it. The dark wooden end tables held porcelain lamps made to look like shepherds and shepherdesses. Fabric lampshades arched above the heads of the figurines. At the opposite end of the room, a giant picture window overlooked the Champs-Elysées. During the rainstorm, the magnificent view looked gray and fuzzy, but Christina was sure that it was spectacular on a sunny day. Next to the window, a graceful marble statue of a girl holding a bouquet of flowers seemed to watch over the room.

"You have an amazing house!" Christina said to Marie.

"Why thank you," she replied. "Jean-Luc and I have lived here all our lives."

"Lucky you!" said Christina.

"Come on, let's get cleaned up and changed," said Marie. "We don't have much time."

She led Christina to the elegant guest bedroom, which was furnished with a four-poster bed and two dressers. A nightstand held an antique clock. The baby blue embroidered bedspread matched the drapes. Christina was sure that she'd have sweet dreams sleeping in a room this beautiful!

"I can't find your suitcases," said Marie, looking a little worried. "The doorman was supposed to deliver them here."

"Uh-oh," said Christina.

"Let's go see if they are in the other room," said Marie in a reassuring voice. "Jean-Luc!" she called. "Have you seen the luggage?"

"We were just about to ask you the same question," he said as he and Grant entered the room. The kids began a search of the whole house. They met back in the living room. The luggage was nowhere to be found!

"Now what?" asked Christina miserably. "We just can't go looking like this! Mimi said that it was a dress-up fancy restaurant, and here we are, soaking wet..."

"...and with pigeon poop in my hair!" interrupted Grant.

The clock struck quarter to seven. "We have to leave now or we'll be late!" cried Jean-Luc.

"But, but," protested Christina and Marie in unison.

"No time for buts!" said Jean-Luc. "We've got a taxi to catch!"

Eerie Elevator

Christina was miserable during the whole taxi ride. She couldn't believe that their luggage was lost! I'm so ashamed to go to the famous Jules Verne restaurant in this dirty outfit, she thought to herself. Here I am in the fashion capital of the world and I look like a ragamuffin, as Papa would say.

"What are we going to do about our clothes for the rest of the trip?" asked Grant.

"I guess we'll have to buy some more if our luggage doesn't show up," said Christina. She perked up a little at the idea of a Parisian shopping spree!

"Cheer up," said Jean-Luc. "We've come this far already. We're following that clue right to the Eiffel Tower. We might even discover the missing statue!"

That is if the Eiffel Tower is still there, thought Christina. She stared out the taxi's window. Rain washed over it in sheets. Thunder rumbled and lightning flickered. Every now and then the wind would blow so powerfully that it caused the raindrops to look as if they were falling sideways. Could the tower really stand such high winds? It looks so tall and thin and unsteady, thought Christina.

She absentmindedly listened to Marie telling about the Jules Verne restaurant and how its chef was one of the finest in the world. After a few moments, the cab pulled up beside the tower. The kids filed out onto the sidewalk, thankfully protected by umbrellas that they had picked up at the apartment.

Christina got her first up-close-and-personal glimpse of the Eiffel Tower. She craned her neck to see all the way to the top, but she couldn't. The lofty spire seemed to disappear into the swirling storm clouds. Christina examined the tower's four massive legs. From far away, they looked so lacy and delicate, but up close, she could see the thickness and strength of each piece of iron that supported that tower. That's a little reassuring, she thought. It looks like a huge, intricate iron puzzle.

There was no more time for admiration. Marie grabbed her hand and dragged her toward the ticket window, where Jean-Luc was purchasing their elevator passes. He handed each person one ticket. "This way," he said, pointing to a distant leg of the tower. "We have to get on the elevator to the second level."

Christina handed her ticket to the attendant, who ripped off one side and handed the stub back to her. She and the others boarded the large elevator car. Another attendant pushed a button to close the doors, and away they went! The car climbed steadily higher until it reached the first level. The attendant opened the door to let more passengers on.

Christina shrieked with alarm. The woman in black was boarding the elevator!! There was no escape this time. She and the others huddled in the corner, frightened by being in such a small enclosed space with this mysterious person! Who knew what would happen next? Christina shivered in her still-damp clothes. Nobody said a word. Lightning flashed and thunder rolled ominously.

After what seemed like an hour, the elevator finally reached the restaurant on the second level. As soon as the doors slid open, pandemonium broke loose! Christina couldn't see too well through all the commotion, but she did make out some policemen who darted onto the elevator and handcuffed the woman in black! She was led off the elevator amid dozens of camera flashes.

"What in the world is going on?" cried Christina, thoroughly confused and a little bit scared. Were the policemen coming for the kids next? She rushed off the elevator, and in her hurry, bumped into someone. It was Mimi! She reached down to give Christina a big, reassuring hug. "We're so proud of you!" cried Mimi.

"What?" said Christina. "Why do you say that? Tell me what's going on!" she pleaded. She looked around to make sure the others were safe. Grant ran to Papa, and Jean-Luc and Marie hugged their parents.

There was still plenty of commotion and yelling as the police herded the woman in black to one side of the room. Newspaper reporters were taking photographs and asking questions at a million miles an hour. Mimi gathered the group together at a large round table. "They caught the statue thief!" she said triumphantly. "The police have been on this woman's trail since early this morning. She and her accomplice specialize in selling precious art from museums around the world. And you kids led them right to her!"

"How...how did that happen?" said Christina.

"Well, I guess you kids caused a little bit of a ruckus at the jewelry counter, the Musée d'Orsay, Notre Dame and the catacombs," Mimi explained. "The guards there called the police to keep an eye on you. As they did that, they saw the woman everywhere you went!"

"So she *was* following us! I was right!" exclaimed Christina.

"What? I don't understand," said Mimi.

"It's a long story," said Grant.

"Well, I do want to hear it," said Mimi. "And I want to find out how you got so messy! But, as I was saying," she continued, "The police discovered that this woman has an accomplice who works with her, giving her hints as to the safest route to smuggle the statue out of the country. They caught the accomplice as he was laying out the trail of clues for the woman to follow."

"Mimi, that's why she was following us!" cried Christina. "We kept picking up her clues!"

"So who is this accomplice?" asked Marie.

"Well, the police already took him off to jail," said Madame Dominique. "But he and the woman had another partner in crime. He is over there!" She gestured to the opposite side of the room.

"Prrr! Prrr!" A familiar cooing sound burst out of a small animal carrier. Christina looked inside. To her surprise, her friend the pigeon was staring back at her with his little beady eyes!

"I just *knew* you were the same bird!" she cried. The pigeon tilted his head.

Madame Dominique walked over to Christina's side. "He is a trained carrier pigeon. His name is Pierre. Evidently, the woman's accomplice sent Pierre to drop off the clues for the woman to find."

"So that's why you're so smart!" Christina said to Pierre. He cooed at her.

"Well, that sure beats all!" said Papa.

"Speaking of bird," said Grant, "Can we maybe *eat* some bird and discuss the rest of this over dinner?"

The Tip-Top of the Tower

Grant pushed his chair back from the table and heaved a sigh of satisfaction. "That was the best meal I've ever eaten!" he declared.

Christina looked up from the gooey chocolate dessert that she was trying to finish. She had been so busy talking during most of the meal that she hardly had time to eat. Now that she had explained how she and the other kids had gotten mixed up in the statue thieves' trail of clues, she attacked her dessert with gusto.

"I'm sorry we look so sloppy," apologized Marie. "We just didn't have time to change clothes."

"It's all right. You children certainly

deserve to be excused after the day you've had," said Cyril.

"Besides, we didn't have any clothes!" interjected Grant. "Our luggage must have gotten lost!"

"Well, if we can't find it, then we might just have to buy some new clothes," said Mimi, winking at Christina. Papa and Grant looked at each other and just shook their heads. "Shopping..." muttered Grant.

"How about taking the elevator up to the observation deck?" asked Cyril. "The storm is almost over, and I'm sure there will be a beautiful view."

"Is it safe to do that?" asked Christina nervously.

"Of course it's safe!" replied Madam Dominique. "Are you frightened of heights?"

"No, it's just that...ummm..." Grant stammered. "We heard that the Tower might blow over in the storm and we didn't want to be stuck on the top when it happens!"

The adults howled with laughter. "That could never happen!" said Cyril. "The tower is designed to sway *with* the winds and withstand them!"

"But we did hear someone say that the Tower was going to fall in this bad thunderstorm," asserted Marie.

"Oh, it was just somebody exaggerating," said Madame Dominique in a reassuring tone of voice. "Don't worry; we are all perfectly safe here."

The kids and adults left the table and boarded the elevator that would carry them to the topmost floor. Christina felt warm and happy inside. They had discovered the statue thieves, and the priceless piece of artwork would be returned to the museum where it belonged, but most importantly of all, the magnificent Eiffel Tower was safe!

The elevator attendant was talking about the construction of the tower. "Construction on the tower began in 1887. The architect, Gustave Eiffel designed the tower for the International Exhibition that was to be held in Paris in 1889. The tower took 300 workers two years to complete. The tower is 300 meters tall and is held together by 2.5 million rivets!"

"Wow!" exclaimed Grant in amazement.

"It takes 40 tons of paint to cover the entire tower," the guide continued. "The tower can also sway up to four inches in high winds."

"There's your explanation," Cyril said to the kids.

"Here we are," said the guide. The elevator doors opened and Christina stepped out onto the viewing deck. The rain had stopped, and the wind whipped through the cool crisp air. She gazed at the incredible view of the city. Lights from the buildings twinkled on the ground, mirroring the twinkling stars in the sky.

"What are you thinking about, Mademoiselle Christina?" asked Mimi.

"I'm thinking about what an unforgettable day this has been," she replied.

"*C'est vrai!*" said Marie. "It is true!"

"So what do you want to do tomorrow?" asked Marie.

"Maybe we could go to the Paris Opera House...you know, the place haunted by the phantom of the opera," said Christina.

"Oh, sure," laughed Marie. "Haven't you had enough of spooky places?"

"After all those skulls and bones today," said Grant, "I'm ready to take on the phantom!" Then he thought for a moment. "But what's a phantom, anyway?"

Everyone laughed. Mimi put her arm around Grant's shoulder and squeezed him tight. "Let's just get a good night's sleep for now," she smiled. "Then we'll see what tomorrow will bring!"

The End

About the Author

Carole Marsh is an author and publisher who has written many works of fiction and non-fiction for young readers. She travels throughout the United States and around the world to research her books. In 1979, Carole Marsh was named Communicator of the Year for her corporate communications work with major national and international corporations.

Marsh is the founder and CEO of Gallopade International, established in 1979. Today, Gallopade International is widely recognized as a leading source of educational materials for every state and many countries. Marsh and Gallopade were recipients of the 2004 Teachers' Choice Award. Marsh has written more than 50 Carole Marsh Mysteries™. In 2007, she was named Georgia Author of the Year. Years ago, her children Michele and Michael were the original characters in her mystery books. Today, they continue the Carole Marsh Books tradition by working at Gallopade. By adding grandchildren Grant and Christina as new mystery characters, she has continued the tradition for a third generation.

Ms. Marsh welcomes correspondence from her readers. You can e-mail her at fanclub@gallopade.com, visit carolemarshmysteries.com, or write to her in care of Gallopade International, P.O. Box 2779, Peachtree City, Georgia, 30269 USA.

Glossary

coincidence: when two or more events seem connected but are not

commotion: a noisy disturbance

embroidered: designs stitched on cloth with a needle and thread

excavate: uncover by digging

gargoyle: a decoration on a building in the form of a strange, imaginary creature

gruesome: causing fear and disgust

hospitality: a friendly and generous way of treating guests

miniature: very small in size or scale

obelisk: a tall stone pillar with four sides and a pointed top

speculate: to think about or make guesses

stammer: to speak in an unsure way, often stopping or repeating certain sounds

Would you like to be a character in a Carole Marsh Mystery?

If you would like to star in a Carole Marsh Mystery, fill out the form below and write a 25-word paragraph about why you think you would make a good character! Once you're done, ask your mom or dad to send this page to:

Carole Marsh Mysteries Fan Club
Gallopade International
P.O. Box 2779
Peachtree City, GA 30269

My name is:______________________________________
I am a:______boy   ______ girl   Age:____________
I live at: ______________________________________
City:____________________ State:____ Zip code:________
My e-mail address: _________________________________
My phone number is: _______________________________

____
____
____
____
____
____
____
____
____

Visit the carolemarshmysteries.com website to:

- Join the Carole Marsh Mysteries™ Fan Club!
- Write a letter to Christina, Grant, Mimi, or Papa!
- Cast your vote for where the next mystery should take place!
- Find fascinating facts about the countries where the mysteries take place!
- Track your reading on an international map!
- Take the Fact or Fiction online quiz!
- Play the Around-the-World Scavenger Hunt computer game!
- Find out where the *Mystery Girl* is flying next!